Heart Strings

Blessings to you and all those you love.
Judith Hennis

JUDITH HENNIS

PAGE PUBLISHING, INC.
New York, NY

First originally published by Page Publishing, Inc. 2018

ISBN 978-1-64214-294-5 (Hardcover)
ISBN 978-1-64214-295-2 (Digital)

Printed in the United States of America

oses traveled with the Hebrew children for forty years through a wilderness. My journey for the past forty years has been with children, age four. In this book, I'll share with you some of the sweetness and some of the pain, some of the laughter and some of the joy of my trip.

One morning, a little boy named Justin and his mama arrived at nursery school. After we said hello, she said, "Tell Mrs. Hennis what happened yesterday." He thought for a moment, and she added, "At the barn."

Then his eyes got real big, and he said, "I was going into the barn, and something big and furry came running out and knocked me down."

His mama said, "It was a groundhog."

"Yeah," said Justin, "and he stole one of my flip-flops."

Then I said, "Well, Justin, I've seen groundhogs sitting beside the road before. So I'll start watching, and if I see one wearing a flip-flop, I'll stop and get it for you."

During free playtime one morning, a little boy who was quite a chunk came hurrying by me, stepping on my foot as he passed. I called his name and said, "Wait a minute. You just stepped on my toes." He just looked at me. I said, "What do you say?" Quickly he said "Thank you" and hurried off to play. I laughed so hard I couldn't even correct him.

While teaching four-year-olds about alphabet, we learned about zebras, which ran up to forty miles per hour. In our town, the speed limit on the road where Pizza Hut was located was forty-five miles per hour. So I told the children to look out their car window when they were passing Pizza Hut and imagine a zebra running in the grass beside them. Then they could understand how fast a zebra could run. A little girl named Tracy went home and told her daddy that zebras ran forty miles to the Pizza Hut. Her daddy really laughed as he told me.

One morning, a little boy named Carson came to nursery school, and he seemed unusually quiet. I asked him if he'd had breakfast and felt his forehead. Then I asked if anything hurt him. He answered, "Yes, I've got a bellyache down to my knees." I gave him a hug, and he walked away toward the cars and trucks. I told the other teacher. A short while later, I left the room to go to the kitchen to put out snack for the morning. Carson's home was directly behind the church, and I saw a moving van parked beside it. Then I knew why his little belly hurt all the way down to his knees—his daddy was moving out.

Jake was a heart-stealer with a very pronounced Southern twang. He came to school on our Halloween party day dressed as Superman. He needed to go potty shortly before the families would arrive. I untied the costume at the back of his neck. He went into the bathroom while I was waiting at the door in the hall for him. Another class teacher came down the hall to ask me a question, and then I heard (remember real Southern drawl), "Missuss Hennus, I need some help." I turned toward him to see my pint-sized Superman scooting his feet, with his white undershirt and underpants, his Superman cape on, and the costume down around his ankles. You know it's not often you get to help Superman dress!

April was a little black girl. Cute as could be and her mama dressed her so cute. One day she was wearing a one-piece jumpsuit. This was during the first two or three weeks in our school year. We had gone to the ladies' bathroom to potty and wash hands before our snack time. There were two enclosed stalls and one sink. I had a girl in each stall and two who didn't need to go potty washing their hands and seven others waiting in line for their turn. April pushed her stall door open and stepped out wearing her panties, with the jumpsuit down around her knees. All the girls looked stunned, but no one said a word. They didn't know that her body was a beautiful dark brown—just like her arms and legs that they'd seen all along in her short-sleeve shirts and shorts. Then I spoke, "Here, April, I'll help you." Then I said, "All you girls are beautiful. God made you that way because He loves you so much!"

One Easter party morning, the children's families came for our egg hunt and party. It was raining hard, so we had to have our egg hunt inside our room. One teacher and I lined up the class and walked them down the hall to go into the church's sanctuary, while parents and the other teacher hid the plastic eggs all over our room (about two hundred eggs). The children sat in the two front pews, and we looked at the lovely stained glass windows. One showed Jesus finding Peter, James, and John asleep in the garden of Gethsemane, and the other showed Jesus speaking to Mary in the garden after the resurrection. A few minutes earlier, I had told the children about Jesus, some of His miracles after He had called men to be His disciples. They heard about the Last Supper, His suffering and death to save us, and that glorious first Easter when He rose from being dead to live again forevermore. When all the eggs were hidden and the children entered our room, they'd been told, "Don't pick up any eggs yet. Wait until you hear 'Ready, set, go.'" At one end of the room, there was a short metal cabinet with a large pot holding a huge jade plant.

Some parent had placed a bright-pink egg in the dirt around the plant. Two children, a boy and a girl, spotted it at the same time and rushed forward to get it. Two little hands shot up together, but the girl was too short to reach it. The boy plucked it out of the pot and, without saying a word, handed it to her and hurried off to find other eggs. This little boy's name was Jansen. I was so touched by his kindness, a little boy being kind like the Precious One we had just learned about.

One morning, I had the boys go to the potty and wash hands for snack time. Two sweet little boys, one black and one white, WT and BJ. This was into our third month of school, and they had become very good friends, playing together. While they were washing their hands, WT, who always seemed so happy and confident, suddenly looked down at their hands, both sets with lots of bubbles. He said, looking at his own palms, "Look, my hands are turning white like yours. I'll bet you'd like me better if I was white all over." My heart was immediately hurting as if it had been pierced. And I said quickly, "WT, we couldn't love you any more if you were white or green or purple. You are perfect just like you are because that's how God made you." I was worried maybe he was insecure inside, underneath his happy-go-lucky exterior. I started to look for some way to reassure him how special he was. Not but a few weeks later, I found a song that I knew God sent me. We taught WT's class and everyone since.

The words said, "Look all the world over. There's no one like me, no one like me. Look all the world over, there's no one like me. There's no one exactly like me. Some people are short and some people are tall. God loves them all. God loves them all. Some people are short and some people are tall, but there's no one exactly like me. Some faces are dark and some faces are light. Each one is special in God's loving sight. Some faces are dark and some faces are light, but there's no one exactly like me." Years later, I came to know his godly mama. I didn't have to worry about WT, but I'm sure God had used that song to help other children since that time.

One year, there was a little blond boy pretending to be a robot during free playtime. Luke was stiffly walking back and forth, moving his little arms like a robot. Then he said, "I am a magic tissing machine. Put in a dime and get a tiss [kiss]." I turned to my friend Carol, the other teacher, and said, "Please loan me five dollars in dimes."

Amanda was her mama's little darling, always dressed like a doll. She had more curls than Shirley Temple. One morning, I had taken the girls to the bathroom to potty and wash hands, before returning to our room for snack time. Two girls were washing their hands while Amanda was at the potty. As she scooted off the potty and reached down to pull up her panties, she said, "Do you like my panties?" (They had lots of ruffles across the back) "They are pink," she said and then asked, "What color are yours?" Before I could think, I answered, "Blue." Then immediately I thought, *Oh my goodness, I'll have to explain this conversation to her mama when she comes today.*

There was a small but very nice zoo about twenty-five minutes away from school. For several years, we made a field trip there to see the animals and birds and enjoy a sack lunch. We traveled in five cars with two adults and five children in each. Parents helped. Three drove their cars, and five rode.

This was many years before seat belts were in cars. Parents had always been so good to help the nursery school. Our trip was always near the end of our school year, and we always had a wonderful time. A precious little girl named Michelle was in class that year. Shortly after our school year began in September, Michelle's mother just left her husband and Michelle. They had no idea where she was. Michelle's dad's parents helped care for her. As we were getting ready to leave the zoo, Michelle, who was in the back of my car, stood up and put her arms around my neck. She said, "Mrs. Hennis, do you know what I wish?" I thought she'd say, "I wish we could come back tomorrow," but she said, "I wish you was my mama."

I said, "Michelle, I love you, and I always will."

The love that God put in my heart for her has blessed both of us. When she was a teenager, her father took his own life. She fell in love a few years later, married, and had a precious daughter. Her husband served in Desert Storm, and she called me to pray for him.

One year we had Tori, Corey, and Lori in the same class with Harry, Carrie, and Mary. I told Carol, the other teacher, if Huey, Dewey, and Lewie showed up, I'd have to leave.

We had a cute little blonde farmer named Caden a few years ago. One morning he said, "I've got a big farm."

My coworker Mrs. Liddle asked, "Well, who helps you on that big farm?"

"My wife," Caden said. "Her name's Shirley."

"Oh," said Mrs. Liddle, "do you all have any children?"

"No," he answered, quickly adding, "but we have five grand-children." He turned around, pointing and saying, "Those three boys and them two girls." Only the really smart ones have the grandchildren first!

Every year we begin to tell the children that our year in nursery school will end soon, but our love for them will never end. We say, "We're glad you had lots of fun here and learned many things. We will be friends forever." A few years ago, on the last day of school, many parents and grandparents were present. We began calling the children's names to come receive their diplomas and get goodbye hugs from all three teachers. One precious little girl named Lauren came when I called her name to get her diploma. We hugged. She turned to hug the other teachers and started across the room to her mama. Then she came running back to me, throwing her little arms tightly around my neck. I held her a moment, saying I'd always love her. When Lauren stepped back, she had tears in her eyes. I smiled at her. She turned around, going toward her mama again. But one more time Lauren ran back to hug me. Then my eyes were also filled with tears. It had gotten so quiet in the room as many of the adults were witnessing her special gift of love to me. I have been so blessed to love and be loved by many children. I'm so grateful to God for this wonderful privilege. I hope I please and honor Him.

For many years our class went to the indoor swimming pool at the local recreation center. A parent or another family member was with each in the water! Our purpose was for every child to have fun. Of course, some boys and girls were afraid of the water and didn't want to get in. We would entice them in several ways. One was to say, "I'll hold you, and we can walk over to see your friend" (who would be paddling around with arm floats or a circle float). We'd watch that one paddling around, and I'd say, "Let's make a train." I'd turn the child I was holding around to hold on to the circle float while I continued to hold them up. Of course, I explained what we were going to do before I began turning the child around in my arms. I'd then tell that one to hold on to the float. Then I'd push the front child's float while holding the second child, turning around to see others having fun. We'd be making train sounds and others would hook on to us, making our train five or six children long. We'd encourage some to sit on the side of the pool, stick their feet in, and splash me.

After a while I'd ask them to stand up and hold my hands while I was in the water, and I'd hold them while they jumped in. I would not let their shoulders go under the water for a few jumps and then later shoulders under but not head. After several minutes of doing this, I'd encourage them to stand up and jump into my arms. I'd catch them and not let their heads go under. Some children I'd take in my arms from their sitting on the steps and walk out in the water. Then I'd say, "We're going to dance," as I began singing "La, la, la, la," etc. and gently bouncing us up and down and twirling around. Then I'd say to someone else who was sitting on the edge, "Look! Amy Cate is dancing in the pool." One cute little boy named Keith was wearing bright-yellow trunks, and he began going up the steps to get out because someone had just jumped in and splashed a lot of water in his face. Trying to distract him and get him to get back in the water, I did gentle little pinches on his shoulders, saying, "There's a snapping turtle in the pool looking for bright-yellow trunks. What color are yours?" He turned around quickly, saying, "They're *blue*!" and continued to grin as he climbed out.

There were two sweet little boys who became fast friends. Their names were Stephen and Mark. Every morning as soon as the last one arrived, they would put on cowboy hats, get on their stick horses, and tell me "Goodbye, we're going to Texas." I'd say, "Have a good trip. See you soon."

Many years ago, there was a soft-spoken little boy named Eli. His daddy seemed so shy and never smiled when we greeted them at arrival time. We only saw his daddy, who never seemed in a hurry, hardly spoke when we said "Good morning" or "Goodbye, see you tomorrow." We thought perhaps he'd had a stroke. Mama came for some holiday parties to see her little boy with his friends. It appeared that Mama had to be the family breadwinner. The last day of our school year, both parents came, bringing Eli. He handed me a small box of Russell Stover candy (four pieces) and a single-stem very wilted chrysanthemum in a small pot. His mama said, "We told him he could choose one gift for you. But he said, 'I really want to give them both to Mrs. Hennis 'cause I love her.'" I was deeply touched because I felt like this family had little but so wanted their little boy to have the experience of nursery school. I planted that tiny wilted chrysanthemum beside my front porch and watered it. It grew to be huge, more than three feet wide and loaded with blooms. It bloomed like that every year, because it was a gift of love. That was twenty-four years ago.

A few years ago, there was a little dark-haired, dark-eyed little girl named Olivia who was so absorbed as I told the class about the first Easter. Only a few days later, she told her mama she wanted to give her heart to Jesus. Olivia's family loved the Lord and had always taken her to church. But her mama said she never dreamed Olivia could be saved at age five, until she and Olivia talked with their pastor. Olivia followed Jesus in being baptized. How wonderful!

Way back in the 1970s, there was a little boy named Brooks who showed us he was a "world traveler." Several children had moved their chairs, making an airplane with their seats. The pilot, who was another little boy, said, "This plane is going to Disney World." Brooks took a seat and said to the others, "Buckle your seat belt and put on your headset." Both Brooks's parents were and still are doctors in our hometown.

Back in the 1980s, a little boy named Kevin was playing in the home area, cooking. He came to me with a pot and a spoon and said, "Would you like to taste my cactus soup?"

"Oh yes," I said. "I've never had cactus soup before, how do you make it?"

Kevin answered, "You put in some hot dogs, some ketchup, some cactus and cook it up." Then I tasted my first ever cactus soup. I told the tiny chef, "It was *delicious*!" Only a few days later, Kevin's daddy opened our classroom door bringing the show-and-tell item Kevin had forgotten to bring that morning. He saw Kevin across the room playing in the home area, holding a baby doll in his arms. His daddy said with dismay, "You let my son play with dolls?" I replied, "He's pretending to be a daddy. Good idea, don't you think?" He smiled then handed me the show-and-tell item and left. Sometime later on, we and our spouses were at a dinner together, when he told those around us about finding his son, Kevin, holding the baby doll and our conversation.

Parents pay tuition at the first of every month. Receipts are given for cash. A sweet little girl named Jackie, who was an only child, was in our class. Her parents were friends of mine at church. One morning, her daddy brought Jackie. She hurried into the room to play. He reached into his back pocket, pulled out his wallet, and opened it. I was thinking and said, "I believe Mama already paid."

He replied, "How much to keep her all day, name your price, it would be worth it."

"Sorry," I replied, laughing, "I don't have enough strength to do all day."

For Christmas, we would take pictures of every child and cut them to fit inside a can lid, making a gold circle around each precious, beautiful face. The teachers had cut from red felt a larger circle with a tab to make an ornament. The children would place their picture on the lid and put the lid on the red felt. Then the child put glue beams and shook gold glitter on the beams.

Earlier on, teachers had cut the red felt and glitter-glued the school's initials and the year on the back side. Of course, every parent was thrilled to get this gift from their child. Shortly after we returned to class from Christmas break, Jackie's daddy said to me, "You know what, you are not a very smart lady. You could have kept those pictures of the children and sold them to us for $20 or more in a few years." It was a joy helping the children to give and feel the joy of giving.

Early on we had a little boy in our class whose name was Travis. He was tall, blonde, with wavy hair, and we couldn't understand a word he said. We tried and tried guessing but were wrong. He'd shake his head and walk away. Of course, the children couldn't understand him either. Carol and I talked about this, not wanting him to be frustrated, and we prayed together and separately to know what to do. The children played with Travis and liked him, even though they couldn't understand him. One morning about mid-year, it was show-and-tell day. Travis had begun to call me "Since" for Hennis, and Carol, the other teacher, "Teach", because he couldn't say Lander.

Another child had brought for show-and-tell a large goldfish swimming around in a Tom's peanut jar with water. There was a special table at the far end of our classroom where we put the show-and-tell things until time to see them. The children could look but not touch until show-and-tell time. When Travis arrived, he had nothing to show, but he noticed the moving fish. He hurried to that table, bent down close to watch the fish, then turned and hurried back to me. I pretended to know nothing. He took me by the hand, saying excitedly, "Uh-mon, uh-mon, Since." (Meaning "Come on, come on, Mrs. Hennis.") I walked with him, asking, "What, Travis?" He kept repeating, "Uh-mon, Since." When we got there, he bent down to look, and I asked, "What is it?" Very strongly he answered, "Shaak!" Shark. I said, agreeing, "It does look like a shark." I knew it was important for him to tell me something, for him to feel right and successful. I thank God for all He has taught me through the children. He leads; I follow. He teaches; we all learn.

There was another cute little boy in the same class as Travis who also had a speech problem, though not as bad as Travis. This little boy's name, that we could understand, was Michael. His mother was a friend of mine. After some time passed, his mama said to me, "I know Michael has a little problem with his speech, but I gather there's another little boy who is hard to understand? Because Michael has said, One boy in my class talks Jackanese." Japanese. His mama laughed and said, "That's the old pot calling the kettle black." Today, Michael is a minister leading a thriving church.

An extremely shy little girl with blonde hair didn't cry when her mama left her the first few days of our school year, but it was easy to see how afraid she felt. Her name was Chrissy. When she arrived, she chose to sit and watch the other children playing. Carol or I would get to sit beside her and talk, telling her how glad we were that she was in our class. We would say, "The girls playing house are cooking. Let's go see what they are making." We'd gently take her hand and walk with her. We would tell the cooks, "This is Chrissy, and we were wondering what you are cooking." We would tell Chrissy their names. We would offer to read a book, but she wouldn't walk to the bookshelf to choose one. We would pick one and read to her. We'd talk about who was in the story and what happened. During music time, we had played Hap Palmer's, What Are You Wearing? Though Chrissy did not sing the chorus with us, she followed every movement.

The next day, Chrissy came in, sat down to watch, and when I sat next to her, she asked, "Will we do that again today?" I wasn't sure what she meant until she said, "What are you wearing?"

I said, "Yes, we will."

That day she smiled as we sang. It became her security blanket, and we did it every day for a long time. We added other songs and finger plays. But all along that remained her favorite. Every year, for forty years, I think of sweet little Chrissy who learned to trust, to feel loved by teachers and classmates, all from playing What Are You Wearing? Now her two little girls are in our classes.

Andy was a cute little blonde boy who would go straight to get a cowboy hat and a stick horse every morning as soon as he came in the door. Then he'd gallop over to me and say, "Gotta go fix the fence. Them cows got out. See you later." Guess what, Andy's a grown man now—with a farm and cows. Sometimes little children are practicing what they will do later.

If only parents knew how important these first five years were, they would live them differently. How many nights does your family eat together at home? Think about this last month. How many stories did your child hear you read? How many games did you play with your precious child? Did you take part in any tickling and giggling? What are your waiting for? Start now! You will forever be glad you did, and so will your wonderful child!

Before our nursery school year begins, we have a get-acquainted meeting night with children, parents, and teachers. We give a handbook to each family and answer questions. The children meet their teachers and play for a while. One parent couldn't attend because of her college class. So she and her son, Austin, came by while we were straightening up. The little boy began to play, pulling out trucks and blocks. The other teacher stayed near him. His mama and I went to a table, and she began to fill out the registration forms. The other teacher began to show Austin the puzzles and books shelf. He walked back to the trucks and blocks he'd been playing with and sat down. Then he looked up at the teacher, smiling, and said, "I'm just coming down here to play. I don't want you to teach me anything." She answered "Okay" and had a hard time not laughing. She told me after they left, and we both had a real good laugh.

Another little boy who was also very self-confident was in our class. Ashton was the darling of his family, adopted and so loved. He became a hero just a short time after our school year ended by calling his daddy at work when his mama collapsed in the floor at home. His mama and daddy had prepared him for this event ahead of time, and Ashton knew exactly what to do. Daddy called 911 and hurried home. Everything turned out well. Every child is a blessing. God uses them to teach us.

Ashley was a little blond girl who didn't have a smile. Before two weeks had passed, we noticed her mama also had no smile. We've always greeted every child first with words and smiles. Then we give those to the adults with them. We never knew why they both were so solemn, but gradually they each warmed up to us. After our school year ended, I received a hand-printed note from Ashley saying she loved me and wanted to come back to help me.

Grumpy became loving—how sweet is that!

In the play-home area, three children were playing. The two little girls were pretending to be Mama and her little girl. Jeffrey, playing the daddy, walked over and opened the oven door. Looking inside, he said, "Honey, your bread's burning." I wish families knew that their children are always watching, always listening. Did you notice he called her Honey? He'd heard that at home.

One special child named Brandi had been born with spina bifida. She was in a wheelchair and was heavy to lift to change her Pampers. Yet it was not a chore but a joy to help her. She was so bright and happy. Brandi loved the other children, and they loved her. She learned a lot at nursery school, and she taught us so much more. Her classmates welcomed her to play with them in the home area. When she wanted to build with blocks down on the rug with other children, we would lift her from the wheelchair. Brandi was so proud of the bright-colored bead balls that her parents had put on her chair's wheel spokes. Her friends wanted to push her down the hall to see and hear the beads move. She loved it, giggling with delight.

Brandi's in heaven now and *not* in a wheelchair.

The morning 9/11 tragedy happened, we were at nursery school. The church's secretary came down the hall to our classroom to tell me what had happened. I quietly told the other teachers in my four-year classroom and went to the other rooms to share the sad news with the other teachers in the three-year and two-and-a-half-year classrooms, asking everyone to pray silently. Protecting the children had always been our first concern. Then I had a very pressing problem to deal with.

Abdul's Mama had talked with me earlier about bringing pizzas for Abdul's class and the other two classes (threes and fours) as a gift. It was a very gracious gift from Abdul's parents, and everyone enjoyed the pizza the week before. I had hurried back to my classroom to call and try to cancel the pizzas, because one parent had said in the hall to other families, "I don't want my child to eat those pizzas." I was so upset. Knowing that Abdul's Mama would be hurt, I tried calling her at home, and at their two business locations. No answer. I told my coworkers I was going to drive to the restaurant to cancel for that day. I drove across town, praying as I went for God to help me, to give me His words. I got to the restaurant and pounded on the door. There were lights on in the back, but no one came to the door or answered the telephone. Then I went back to school and waited for Abdul's Mama to arrive with fourteen pizzas. She was pregnant with her second child, and I was so worried about her. I was praying all this time. When she drove into the church parking lot, I hurried out the door, calling her by name. I went to her, placing my hands gently on her arms and saying, "Oh, Dooah, I am so sorry, but we cannot accept the pizzas today." By that point, we were both crying. (I'm crying now as I write this.) I embraced her, saying some of the parents were upset and didn't want their child to have the pizza. I said, "I know they meant no harm. And my heart is breaking because I know this is hurting you." We hugged again, and she got in her car and drove away. The next day after school, I talked with the pastor, Reverend Conley. He had been out of town the day before. He listened and told me he thought I'd done the right thing. He expressed his sympathy to me, and being the very kind man he was, he called Abdul's family to offer to let them come stay in the parsonage with him if they felt unsafe. The next day, I went to their restaurant and asked if I could talk with Abdul's father and mother.

Again, I told them how very sorry I was. I repeated to Abdul's father what I done and said the previous day, expressing my sorrow that they had been hurt. Abdul was returned to nursery school for the rest of our school year. Just a few months later, Abdul's Mama gave birth to a beautiful little girl. I visited with Mama in her hospital room, bringing a gift for the baby.

Daddy arrived, and we all smiled and talked about the beautiful baby. Abdul's family and I remain friends today.

I have an unusual pin that shows giraffes and zebras running together. I wear it every year when my nursery school class of four-year-old children are learning about the alphabet. To make the study of letters, their sounds, and how to make them more interesting, we teach one animal, bird or fish daily. We would teach where the animal lived, what it ate, how many babies it had, and so on. We would say there were no mean animals, but some animals were meat eaters, so they had to kill other animals to eat. It was all part of God's plan to take care of everything He had created. His plan was always best. If lions ate grass like the zebras did, soon there would be too many zebras and lions eating grass. And then both groups would die, starving. Zachary, a cute little blond-headed boy, was shopping with his mama one day out of town. When he spotted that giraffes and zebras running pin, he said, "Oh, Mama, I need to take that pin to

Mrs. Hennis. She told us they ran together to be safe, and they are friends." Over and over during our school year, we would say, "God has a wonderful plan. He made us. He loves us and will always take care of us."

Speaking of animals running, I remember Betsy, who was always talking about her horse, Bravo, and her three brothers. Dan and Todd were twins, and the baby was Keith. Betsy reminded me of my own dear daughter, Ann. Both girls were sweet and kind to everyone, and strong and gentle. One day, Betsy came to school just bubbling over.

"Guess what, Mrs. Hennis, Mama came walking through our house, and there stood Bravo right in our dining room. Someone left the sliding door open."

Sometimes children remind me of someone from the past. Well, I've had both John Wayne and Hoss Cartwright in my class, but not at the same time. John Wayne (a.k.a. Conner) had perfect posture, was tall and built strong, with broad shoulders. He never seemed to be in a hurry. He enjoyed watching other children play, as well as playing himself. He was always kind to everyone. As for Hoss Cartwright (a.k.a. Luke), he was built like the real Hoss Cartwright, with some extra padding around his middle. He loved to laugh. Every day he wore cowboy boots that were well-worn. Our class had learned a song about five little chickadees during winter. I had showed the children pictures of chickadees. We talked about what they ate, how they flew, and how they sang. We did hand motions as we sang and counted backward from five to one and then none. Luke asked many days, "Please, can we sing the 'Chicken Bee' song?" as he called it.

Recently I was eating lunch at Subway, when a couple was in line to order. She glanced my way and said, "Are you Mrs. Hennis?"

I answered, "Yes."

She said, "You had my son, John, in nursery school twenty-five years ago. Recently we were talking about living in Galax. Then he said, 'I still remember the chickadee song we sang. Mrs. Hennis told us we were like chickadees, both small and very happy when it's snowing.'"

We both smiled and hugged before saying goodbye.

Last year, the first day back to school after Christmas, I was asking each child at circle time what they had wanted for Christmas. A boy named Riley, who was always low-key and mild-mannered, when asked the question, he answered "God" in a very soft voice. I said, "Oh, Riley, I know God loves you. He's smiling right now, and He will never leave you." The next time I saw his mama, I asked if their family went to church anywhere. She told me they'd been going about six months and called the church name. I told her what Riley had said and told her, "You might want to tell the pastor. I believe God is moving in Riley's heart."

The Methodist Church asked the teachers at nursery school to have our classes sing before the church congregation in just two weeks. So both the three-year and four-year classes took turns going into the sanctuary to practice our songs. At the end of the morning, Mrs. Myers, a three-year teacher came to my classroom to tell me what had happened at their practice time. Mrs. Myers had told me they had the children lined up near the pulpit and she noticed one little boy, named Travis, who kept looking at the door near the back of the sanctuary and smiling. After the children had practiced two songs, Travis, who continued looking and smiling, waved. Mrs. Myers looked toward the door, but no one was there or anywhere in the large sanctuary. Then she said, "I know what you'd say—that he saw Jesus or an angel." Travis was a precious Down syndrome three-year-old. I believe every child with special needs has a unique awareness of Jesus's presence. No wonder they smile—they see His loving smile!

One morning during our free playtime, a boy named Elijah suddenly called out from the center of the room. He yelled, "Help! I can't swim! I'm on a rock in the middle of the river!" I said, "Hold on, Elijah, I'll save you." Then I stooped down and picked up a pretend rope, swinging it like a lasso over my head. After circling the lasso a few times, I pretended to throw it. I shouted, "Catch it, Elijah, and hold on tight. I'll save you!" He grabbed the pretend rope. I pulled hard, hand over hand. Elijah, holding the pretend rope, walked out of the river, smiling.

The children (twenty-two of them) stood still watching. Elijah looked proud. If only I could have saved him from the turmoil in his family. Elijah's dad had just told his mama that he was gay.

One year a few days before Christmas, a little boy named Shawn came to nursery school carrying a small package wrapped in Christmas paper. When I said, "Good morning, Shawn," he replied, "My mama said don't tell you—it's bafume." Then he quickly handed this gift to me and hurried on to play. It was perfume. I told her about that episode many years later, and she laughed. A couple of months later, Shawn came to school, accompanied with his daddy, who always brought him and picked him up. He walked to another boy and drew something out of his pocket. I went to see what it was, because children were not supposed to bring anything to school except on show-and-tell day. The teacher at the classroom door greeting children and family members would take the show-and-tell item and put it up until show-and-tell time.

What Shawn had taken out of his pocket was a knife, a switchblade knife! You know, you touch the button and the blade flies out. I was so surprised and quickly took it away from him.

I asked, "Where did you get this?"

"It's my daddy's," he answered.

I knew both Mama and Daddy and had for a long time. We attended the same church. Of course, I spoke privately with Daddy when he came to pick up Shawn. He apologized. I had earlier talked with Shawn, explaining he could have gotten hurt or accidentally hurt another child. The other teacher and I thanked God for His wonderful protection of all our children all the time.

Our four-year classes used to make many field trips in the spring. We were at a friend's dairy farm, in the barn. We came to see the milking. One cow at the far end of the line suddenly began to have a very loose bowel movement. The other teacher, Mrs. Mitchell, was at that end. She quickly turned her back to the cow, fanning out her jacket on both sides to protect the children's faces. Of course, it hit her jacket. When we thanked the farmer for letting us visit and watch as he milked the cows, we went to the church's van. Mrs. Mitchell removed her jacket, turned it inside out, and put it on the van floor. We helped the children get into the van, seat-belted everyone, and drove away. Mrs. Mitchell asked the children if they had enjoyed seeing the cows get milked. Karen, a tall blonde girl, spoke right up, saying, "That cow really pooped on us. It did. It really pooped on us."

Many, many years ago, a boy named Keegan came to our school, accompanied every day by his grandpa. Keegan was an only child. He loved coming to nursery school and playing with all our toys, blocks, trucks, and puzzles. That year, our enrollment number was down, which of course meant less money going into our budget. Before our first month ended, Keegan's grandpa brought a large bag filled with cookies, chips, and juice jugs and handed it to me. He said, "These are for Keegan's class." I said, "Thank you, but you don't have to bring snacks. The school pays for them." He continued all year long, every month, to bring his sack full of goodies. God supplies all our needs, just as He promises in His Word. How often God prompts us to help someone, and when we listen and obey, that someone is blessed. And so are we.

So many times families have seen a way they could help us and very kindly responded.

Very early on, probably thirty-five years or more ago, Margo was brought to nursery school by her Aunt Laura. Margo's Mama was a schoolteacher. Snack supplies were kept down the hall from our classroom in the church's nursery, where we used a cabinet and refrigerator. Aunt Laura, walking by the door and holding Margo's hand, saw me struggling to open a can (all metal) with one of those old can openers. The kind you forced the blade down into the can's lid and turned and turned the handle with one hand keeping the opener in place. To mix Kool-Aid was an effort. The next day when Margo and Aunt Laura came to school, Laura handed me an electric can opener. She said she and her sister, Margo's mama, wanted us to have it. It worked perfectly all the years after that until our school had to close. I never used it that I didn't remember Margo, her mama, and Aunt Laura and of course God, who supplies our every need. I thanked Laura on the spot, wrote a note, and mailed it to her sister and thanked her.

Can you imagine the nickname Worm? It surprised me many years ago, when I heard a tall mama call her little girl that. The child's name was Sarah, a happy girl who enjoyed the other children and every activity every day. I never asked her mama why she called Sarah "Worm." I've heard people say to a child they were holding in their arms, "Stop being a wiggle worm."

But guess what, Sarah's all grown up now, and for several years, she's been working at our city's library as the children's librarian. With joy and enthusiasm, she does story hour weekly for toddlers through preschoolers. She leads them in songs and finger plays. She helps them with art activities that they can proudly carry home to show Mama, Daddy and grandparents. She's planting seeds in their hearts to love books. That will make them eager to learn to read, and that's the beginning of being an outstanding student. So you see, Sarah's mama was right. Sarah was a happy worm who became a happy bookworm as an adult.

It's so easy to see the love many parents have for their child. In all my forty-two years, one couple stood out. They came together every day all year to bring their son, Zackary, and to pick up at noon. He didn't cry, but you could see he was awfully close, and so was Mama. We would help him begin to play with some toys, or we would do the clown-balancing puzzle with him.

The clown would stand, straddling a bicycle, and holding both hands up. Then you could choose pieces to balance on his hands and his head. There was an umbrella and two balls (different colors). Every morning at the start of the school year was the same for him, no crying but right on the verge during the first part of our morning until he settled in comfortably. Zackary really loved our school after he got over the hurdle. We always reassured tearful children, saying,

"Your [blank] will be here to pick you up at the lunchtime." (Fill in the blank with Mama, Daddy, Grandma, Grandpa, Papa, babysitter, etc.) About the fifth or sixth morning, Zackary turned his head and looked at me, saying, "I don't know why this water keeps coming out of my eyes." I answered, smiling at him, "I know why, Zackary. It's because this is a new thing, and doing a new thing always makes us feel a little scared, until we find out everything's okay. I think you are having fun here every day, playing with our toys, hearing stories, learning songs and games, and making friends. You know Mama and Daddy want you to be happy while you are here. I think today will be the last day that water comes out of your eyes." And guess what? It was.

We had a little blond-haired girl named Briana who came to school every day looking like someone had used one of those old-timey eggbeaters instead of a hairbrush on her hair.

That happened all year long. Later on, I was told that Grandma went to pick up Briana and her brother Lucas and take them to school each day. Their mama didn't want to get up until the last minute to go to work.

Then there are those mamas who go all the way for their own child. One year, two months before our school year would end, a mama with a sad look on her face told me her little boy would have to drop out. Mama was changing jobs the next week and would not have any way to get her sweet little boy to school because she had to be at her new job earlier. She said, "I'm so sorry, because Tate loves it here. He has learned so many good things." Standing behind Tate's mama was Aiden's mama. Aiden had wiggled past them to get inside to play. Tate and Aiden, of course, were good friends. Then lovingly, without hesitation, Aiden's mama, Angie, said, "You can bring him to my house, and I'll take them to nursery school."

"Oh, that would be wonderful!" Tate's Mama exclaimed. "How much would you charge?"

"Oh, nothing," Aiden's mama replied.

They continued walking down the hall together, talking. And Tate came to school, completing our year, with his friend Aiden, much to our joy. Remember I said many mamas go all the way for their own dear child. And a truly loving servant of our Lord Jesus will go out of their way to help another child.

On some occasions, parents disappointed me. During the whole month of December, we (all the teachers and I) sought to help the children think about Jesus. We said, "We wouldn't have Christmas if God had not sent Jesus to come to earth and be born as a baby. Jesus was the first and best Christmas present." All month long we kept telling the children, "We're going to have a birthday party for Jesus right here at school. You know how when it's your birthday, you have a cake or a cupcake with candles on it? The candles are burning, and you make a wish and blow out the candles, after everyone sings 'Happy Birthday' to you. That day you are the only one who gets to make a wish and blow out the candle. Well, on Jesus's birthday, He wants all of you to have a candle so all of you can make a wish, sing 'Happy birthday, Jesus,' and blow out the candles." I would say, "Every time I see a candle burning, I remember that Jesus is the light of the world." I would say to all the grown-ups present, "Look at these precious little faces in the candlelight and remember this beautiful moment."

I always asked the parent who wanted to bring the party refreshments to not bring anything with Santa Claus, Rudolph, etc. to eat or on the plates and napkins. We wanted the children to focus on Jesus. I asked for cupcakes, white, yellow, or rainbow (no chocolate—way too messy for party day!) with white icing. It was okay if families brought Santa or Rudolph treat bags for the children to take home. One year, the mama who'd said she'd bring the cupcakes arrived carrying a tray. She was so pleased with herself, saying, "When I saw these in a magazine, I just had to bring them for my son's party." They were chocolate no-bake cookies for the face, pretzels for the antlers, and half a maraschino cherry for the nose, raisins for eyes.

Rudolph! I could have cried on the spot. If you are that mama reading this, I forgive you, because I've been forgiven for so much worse things.

Another Christmas, a daddy had been told by mama to pick up decorated cupcakes at the grocery store's bakery and take them to their son's teachers for the party at eleven o'clock. He was in the three-year-olds class with two teachers. The daddy went to the grocery store and bought a five-pound sack of Florida oranges, saying, "These are for the party." No cupcakes.

One teacher came to my classroom, saying, "Now, what do I do? We need to practice our Christmas songs, have our story, and take the children to the potty before the families come."

I said, "Go to our kitchen and get the store-bought Christmas cookies we offer to our family members present for the party and serve them to the children along with the oranges. Our aide will cut them into wedges that the children can hold and eat."

I don't know if that mama ever knew what happened, because no one from that child's family attended.

That makes me think of another cupcake story. It was our Easter party day, and families had been invited to hear the real story of Easter, hear the children sing the songs they had learned, and enjoy refreshments with us. The other teachers and I were busy serving the children, when I saw a daddy cross the room, help himself to a cup of apple juice, and pick up a frosted cupcake. He took a step or two and dropped the cupcake, frosting down on the floor. He stepped back, setting his juice cup on the teacher's table. He then picked up the cupcake, dusting off the top, and walked to where his wife was chatting with another mama. He handed her the dusted-off cupcake and went back to get another one for himself.

Right after my son, Christopher, graduated from Virginia Tech with a degree in communications, he was hired as a dispatcher for the Grayson County Sheriff's Department. He met an officer named Darren, and they asked each other, "Do you have children?"

Then Darren said, "I have a beautiful little girl named Beth. She's four."

Christopher said, "Oh, then you should get her signed up to be in my mom's nursery school class. She loves those kids, and they love her. And they learn so much."

Darren quickly replied, "Oh, no. I'm not sending my little Beth to any school. I'd like to keep her home till she's about fifteen."

A few days later, Chris mentioned it again, saying, "You'd better call. They fill up quickly."

Darren emphatically answered with a little grin on his face, "No, I'm not sending my sweet little Beth to your Momma's boot camp."

Chris told me about their conversations. And a short time later, Beth's mama called to sign her up, saying she'd have to talk Daddy into it. Beth came, loved it, and midway through the year, so did Dad.

I've seen a lot of caring daddies and wonderful mamas down through the years. And I've noticed two special groups of daddies who not only love their children, they cherish them. By cherish I mean they are more aware of everything about their child. Perhaps the nature of their jobs has made them more aware of the precious blessings—their child. One group is dairy farmers, such long hours, 7 days a week, 365 days a year. The other group is police officers, who know the unforeseen dangers that could in a moment snatch them away from their loved ones. Don't ever say to your child, "Hurry up and say your prayers." Take time, cuddle them inside a warm hug, bow your head, listen to their prayer, then speaking out loud, thank your wonderful Father for your daughter or son and all your family. Thank Him for always loving us. Kiss your precious one good night. If that doesn't fill you up with love, something's wrong.

Sometimes things in life are so wrong, so painful that we almost lose sight of the truth that God always works things to our good, in His time. I saw this just a few years back. We had a darling little boy, Colton, in our two-year class. Colton had a baby brother, Caleb, just a few months old, and a big sister, Katie. One evening I learned that Colton's daddy had taken his own life. I was crushed hearing it. I knew that fine young man, his sweet wife, and all four grandparents. On my way to their home, I prayed and prayed. When I got there, Colton's grandma (his mama's mama) let me in. We hugged. Then she took me to the bedroom to see Jenny. We held each other, crying, and I prayed to the God of all comfort for help. I prayed for help for Jenny, her children, her parents, and his parents. His parents and I had graduated from high school together. I knew their hearts were broken. That was one of the saddest times in my life. About two weeks later at nursery school, Colton's teachers came to my classroom to tell me that during that morning, Colton had said, "My daddy's picking me up today." They said, "We felt like crying. It hurt so bad." Then they got him to play. A few years later, Jenny began to spend time with another fine young man, James. James had never been married. I'd known him since he was a child. His dear parents had been my friends at church for many years. From the very first of Jenny and James's relationship, James reached out to Colton, Katie, and Caleb with gentleness and love. In time, they became engaged and married. It was the most touching wedding I've ever seen. After James and Jenny were at the altar, along with Katie (her mama's maid of honor) and Colton (beside James with Caleb, the ring bearer), James asked the three children to sit with him on the steps up to the altar. He faced Katie and Caleb with Colton beside him. Then he told them he loved their mama and he loved them. He told them he did not want to take their daddy's place. That he knew they would always love their daddy. And now he wanted to be a part of their family, to love them along with their mama. There was not a dry eye in that church! And I was praising God over and over in my mind as my heart was overflowing with love for my amazing Father. What love the Father has bestowed on us! Later at the lovely reception that James had prepared, he told me that all down through the years, he had wondered why he couldn't find the woman he would love. And now he knew why God had him waiting.

They've been so happy now, all five of them, for many years. Thank you, God, for your faithfulness to keep all your promises.

During the first seven years at nursery school, I worked with a wonderful woman, Carol Lander. God put us together and greatly blessed us as we worked. We didn't know each other. She belonged to the Methodist Church, and I belonged to the Baptist Church. My children, Ann and Chris, attended Bible school at the Methodist Church with their cousins, James and Gray.

And then James and Gray would come to the Baptist Bible School. One day I went to pick up my children and saw a group of little children playing games out in the church yard. There was a beautiful little dark-haired girl wearing a white sundress with flowers and butterflies stitched on the bodice. I asked whose child she was, and a lady said, "She's Carol Landers's." A month earlier, I had gone to the Methodist Church to see Reverend Nelson Woody to ask if I could be an aide or a substitute teacher in the nursery school. He had hired me to be a teacher. I thought I'd be joining the two teachers who were already there, Jean Cook and Myrna Holder. But Reverend Woody told me they were both leaving for other jobs, and another teacher would be hired. So mid-June when I saw pretty little Margaret, I called her mama and introduced myself over the phone. I said, "I would like to meet you. My daddy works at Burlington Mills here where Margaret's daddy does." I told her about seeing Margaret playing at Bible School and asking whose child she was. Then I told her about being hired to teach at nursery school. So I went to Carol's house the next afternoon, taking my Ann, age nine, and Chris, age four. We became friends immediately, because our hearts were the same. We deeply loved Jesus and our children.

Carol's children, Tommy and Margaret, were one year younger than Ann and Chris. The four of them played together and never had a cross word, while Carol and I worked together many afternoons that summer of 1973. We used a set of Compton's Encyclopedias for children to choose what we'd teach the children. The Children's Compton's Encyclopedias had been a gift from Carol's mama. The two ladies who had previously taught, of course, did colors, shapes, counting, alphabet, with their one class of eighteen children three mornings weekly. But Carol and I wanted to do even more.

As we thumbed through the pages of the children's encyclopedia, one of us would say, "Oh, bees! Kids would love learning about bees. And we could let them taste honey on a plastic spoon. For art, we can draw a beehive on gray construction paper that they can cut out and glue on a light-blue construction paper for the sky. We need to have a finished example for display that they can look at while they are working. Then they can glue five bees around or on the hive. Of course, we'll have to draw and cut out the bees from yellow construction paper. And then last, the children can use a brown crayon to draw the tree branch that holds the hive."

We made notes of animals to teach and added them to the alphabet study. We taught that God made all the animals, birds, and fish in our world and that He gave them everything they needed. They learned where each one lived, what it's babies were called, what they ate, who its enemies were, and how it could protect itself and its family. Our school year began in September, the day after Labor Day, and ended in May, just before Memorial Day. Remember, we were only going three mornings a week, but in a year's time, our classes learned about camels, bears (black, polar, grizzly, brown), elephants (African and Asian), giraffes, kangaroos, lions, monkeys, peacocks, tigers, whales, zebras. I knew all this was God directed, because it was joy-filled for Carol and for me. It was never a chore. It was such an amazing pleasure, because we were helping the children (four-year-olds) to see God, the Creator. It is never too early to teach children about God. You should say to your tiny baby, "You are a blessing given to me and Mama (or Daddy) by God. I love you so much, and God loves us even more." God will pour wonderful blessings into your life if you seek to raise your child to know Him.

While Carol and I worked to establish lesson plans, we chose seasons, American Indians and Thanksgiving (November), Christmas, Easter, community helpers, our five senses (seeing, hearing, smelling, tasting, touching), counting and number recognition and alphabet. Working together, we handwrote all we'd teach, songs we'd sing, finger plays and art (to color, cut, glue, paint). Please remember this, when Carol and I began, there were no curriculum books, only art, music, and finger plays. But no doubt about it, God was leading. You see, more than twenty years later, the church encouraged the teachers at nursery school to pursue early childhood classes at our local community college. Guess what? The curriculum subjects were numbers (counting and recognition), alphabet (phonics and recognition), community helpers, seasons, five senses, exactly what God had led us to. Carol and I worked together for seven years, until her husband was transferred to Burlington, North Carolina. The day she moved was one of the saddest days of my life. Early on in our time working together, I jokingly said, "You know what, this is getting so good people are going to start calling us from the hospital when their baby is born to sign them on our list." We both laughed. I know now God laughed too. You see, within the next three years, I received a call from Birmingham, Alabama. The lady said, "I'm calling to get my son, Will, on the list for your class. We'll be moving to Galax soon. My husband will be working in radiology at your hospital." Soon after that, I got a phone call from Eaue Claire, Wisconsin. The lady said, "I want to enroll my son, Robert, in your nursery school class. My husband is a doctor, and we'll be moving Galax." Also, the call from the hospital came to sign up Ben on the list for four years later. All three boys came.

God grew and grew nursery school from one class of four-year-olds. The year my daughter, Ann, would enter college, I was approached by a friend from my home church, First Baptist–Galax, offering me a job in his very successful real estate and insurance business. While I loved nursery school and my friend and new coworker, Linda, I knew I could earn a lot more money if I took that job. Money that would help my family with college expenses, but my heart was so happy at nursery school. I prayed, "God, what should I do?" Over and over I asked Him. Then the answer came in my head, "*Grow where you are.*" I knew what God meant—add another class. He had already provided the names and the phone numbers of the families. I was so excited, so happy that I cried with joy. The next morning I called Reverend Hudson to make an appointment to talk with him. I told him from the beginning to end what had happened. I asked if we could have a second class for four-year-olds to meet on the other two mornings each week. I said I'd ask Linda if she would like to work five mornings or stay at three. If she didn't want to work five mornings, we could hire another teacher. Reverend Hudson was so pleased and gave his immediate approval. He stated the nursery school was a wonderful blessing to children and their families. We planned for me to draft a letter to the families on the list, telling them about the new class for the fall. The letter stated we'd call in two weeks for registration. I called Linda, and she agreed to work five mornings. When we called families, the class (both classes, now a three-morning and two-morning) were filled. God is so amazing. He blesses in so many ways, to so many people (all ages, all races). It's like an avalanche—so overwhelming! He was *the* multitasker, before any person thought up that word.

During the first seven years that Carol and I had worked together, we came upon a problem, a serious problem. Our enrollment was too low. We had only sixteen children enrolled a month before our school year would begin. We needed seventeen to buy snacks and pay our salaries. Our working supplies (tissues and art things) had already been purchased. So Carol and I talked and decided we would each take a $25 pay cut. It doesn't sound like much, but we only made $150 for the month. So that's how our year began. Two months later, the seventeenth child was enrolled. And one month after that, number eighteen came. Sometime later on, we talked about how God provided what we needed. We realized that it had just been a test. What were we there for?

What we could give the children—love, patience, kindness, lessons—or what we carried home in our paychecks.

Let's talk about twins, twice as cute, right? The first set were two little blond-haired girls with round faces I'd never met. Their mama signed them up and said their aunt would be bringing them. She thought they'd do better with her. Our class was located three rooms from the outside door. You could hear them screaming in stereo the minute the three of them came in the door. It sounded like they were being skinned alive. It took a few minutes to get both Erin and Catie interested in playing, but then they were fine. They cried again the next morning for a very short time and then had a great time. Then came Garrett and Gavin, identical with almost little pixie faces and so small and sweet. Then came Ben and Bobby, dark-haired, brown-eyed, slim, and so quiet. Later we had a set of twins you could tell apart, Heather and Nathan. A few years later, we had Dan and Todd. I always guessed the wrong name when I talked to them. I could never tell who was who. Then came a set of twins I could tell apart, Sarah and Allison. Sarah was a couple of inches taller than her sister, Allison. Sarah was the leader of the two. A few years later, Clare and Hallie came to our class. Two little blond heads with tight corkscrew curls. More curls than Shirley Temple, and just as cute. The last set of twins were Troy and Luke. They said "Twahwe" and "Wuke." They were your regular little boys, but they had such tender little hearts when someone got hurt. When another boy fell because he tripped on some blocks, they hurried over and reached down to help him, saying, "You all right, widdow buddy?" We saw this on more than one occasion, and it warmed our hearts. All the twins we had made me think of that old line "double the pleasure, double the fun." They all certainly were.

Many years ago, we had one set of triplets, Rachel, Emily, and Milo, each one unique and so different from each other, in looks and interests.

One morning I was in the church office running some copies for art when the church secretary answered the phone and said it was a call for nursery school. I answered and the lady said she wanted to get her child into the school. Her little girl, Ashley, was four years old but could not walk or talk. She'd been born with cerebral palsy. I said she'd be welcome. I believed anyone Jesus sent, He'd help us to help in some way. This was mid-way through our year.

Ashley joined us in February. Her mama brought a beanbag chair for Ashley to sit in. She was unable to sit in a regular chair. She had no sense of balance. She could say two words, *Mama* and *bye*. At free playtime, we would put Ashley in her beanbag chair with a doll or plastic blocks in her lap. At times we would hold her in our lap and read stories to her. We would play Pat-a-Cake with her while holding her on our lap many times. Then we would say, "Let's stretch this arm way up high and now this arm." We would hold Ashley in our lap with one hand and place our other hand over hers as we rolled a truck back and forth on the tabletop. We'd say, "Here goes the truck—*broom*—and here it comes back—*beep beep beep*." Then one morning I had the idea to make a train with children down on hands and knees that Ashely could see. After our train circled around Ashley twice, I placed Ashley down on the rug on hands and knees. I straddled her, placing my hands on her wrists to move her arms and hands. The other teacher, Mrs. Mitchell, hooked another little girl behind Ashley with her hands on Ashley's ankles to move her feet. Ashley liked it! We were making choo choo sounds as we slowly moved around on the rug. She was grinning ear to ear. Our school year ended right before Memorial Day, and Ashley came to our four-year class again in September the day after Labor Day. She stayed with us all year, and all the children in both classes were incredibly kind to her. Midway through the second year, Ashley began talking to us in five-word sentences.

There were others that had difficulties in life, and each one was and is precious—Molly, Jeremy, and Julie. Each one was born into such loving families who would help them to be all they could be.

It was easy to see the amazing talents God had poured into some children. The little artists who drew free hand and colored their masterpieces were Zachary, Joyce, and Tianna. I believe Mrs. Liddle, a teacher alongside me, was one who watered the seeds God had put there in four-year-olds' hearts. She had and still has a wonderful warm heart that draws children like a magnet. Many who were not interested in doing art when the class did became intrigued and wanted to do something a few others were doing with Mrs. Liddle during free playtime. Our exceptional musicians were Morgan, playing her tiny fiddle, and three sisters who each sang beautifully. Of course, they came three different years. Their names were Kaitlyn, Meagan, and Autumn. They sing at churches now.

Many years ago, there was a little girl named Iva in our class. Iva's daddy said one spring morning, he would like to bring a sheep to show Iva's class, and he wanted to shear the sheep outside while we watched. He said he could come the next morning. I said, "That would be great." So the next morning he came bringing Iva and the sheep named Isabella. Isabella weighed 156 pounds. Iva's daddy had brought a sturdy bench to sit on, as he lifted the sheep's front legs up and leaned her body back to rest against him. His legs cradled the sheep's sides. Isabella did not struggle. She knew and trusted this shepherd. You see, sheep would be miserable wearing that heavy coat of wool during the hot months of summer. God causes the sheep to grow another thick wooly coat before winter comes again, to keep them warm. Iva's daddy explained each thing he would do before he began. I had introduced Iva's daddy, and he had told them about Isabella first. Our children stood in a semicircle to watch. I had never seen a sheep up close or the shearing. Then Iva's daddy turned on the shears and began to move it down Isabella's tummy. After he had cut away a large section all in one piece, he cut off the shears and laid them down. Then he let us step up two children and one teacher at a time to touch the thick wool on one side and the lanolin on the underside. It was amazing to children and teachers.

There were so many amazing experiences God brought us at nursery school to teach us all how He cares for this world. We often told the children God made everything that was good. He loves and cares for the animals, the birds, the fish. But His absolute favorite is you and every man, woman, child, and baby. His love lasts forever.

Kelby, how sweet, gentle, and kind to others he was. Kelby stuttered, but he never got impatient or angry with anyone. I think God gave him an extra portion of grace to be shared with others.

Several of the children at nursery school came from foreign lands. Amy was born in Korea, adopted and brought to Galax, Virginia, by her parents. Misha was born in India. His mother was born in England and his father in India. His family moved to Galax, Virginia, also. Rachel's mother who lived here in Galax traveled to China to live for three weeks, as required to adopt a child there. I remember seeing Rachel as a tiny baby in Mama's arms. Today, I see Rachel as a beautiful cheerleader for Maroon Tide Sports (Galax High School). Then there was Molly, whose parents and older brother, Corey, lived here in Galax. Molly's daddy flew to Guatemala to get Molly when she was only five and a half months old. I remember seeing her a short time later. How very fortunate both Rachel and Molly were to have been adopted into such loving families. The last child was Gerardo, born in Mexico. He was shy but smart and spoke English well. All these children loved being in our school. They learned much and made lasting friends.

During the first few years of teaching preschoolers, a little boy named Will went home and told his Mama something shocking. He said, "Guess what, Mama, today at school we painted on weasles. My picture was still wet. I can bring it home tomorrow." Will's Mama, being a schoolteacher, knew the weasel was really an easel.

A little boy named Eli was brought to school by his grandpa. His older brother, Travis, was about twelve. Both were soft-spoken, good little boys. Eli's favorite thing was to build with the blocks. One morning I was nearby as he played. When his tower of blocks

39

fell, I heard him softly say the *S _ _ _* word. I was shocked! I told the other teacher, saying I thought I heard that word but wasn't sure. I asked her to help me listen for the next few days. In just a couple of days, the same scenario played out. Eli's block tower building, blocks tumbling over, and that word softly said. I walked over and sat down near him. I said, "Eli, you just said a word that's not a good word for people to say." I was watching his face to see if he knew what word I was talking about. He knew.

I said, "I saw your blocks tumble over, and I know you were disappointed. I know a good word you can say when something goes wrong. It's *shucks*. Can you say *shucks*? Let me hear you." When he said it, I said, "Good, say it again. That other word that's not good to say means when your grandpa's cows do poop outside. It's dirty and smells bad. That's why it is not a good word. Do you remember the good word you can say instead?"

Eli answered, "Shucks."

"Very good, Eli, you are such a smart boy. I know you'll remember."

A couple of days later, same scenario. When the blocks fell, he said "S——" and then quickly turned to look at me while saying "Shucks!" I smiled at Eli and said, "Good remembering, I'm proud of you!" I received a warm smile. I never again heard that wrong word.

About two weeks after our school year ended, Eli and his brother, Travis, went fishing with their grandpa at Byllesby Dam, just a few miles from Galax. Appalachian Power Company had a substation located there. People in our area had always said there were fish in that dam five feet long. Eli was sitting on a large flat rock, holding his fishing pole, and he was jerked into the water. He could not swim. His grandpa, who also could not swim, yelled to Travis to "run, get help." Then Grandpa jumped in. Both Grandpa and Eli drowned that day. What a heartbreaking day that was. I went to the hospital to see Eli's parents, but when I arrived, they were in a private area with a minister. A nurse who knew me came to me and asked if she could give me Eli's clothes to take to his parents later on. She said she thought that would be best. I nodded with tears in my eyes and took the gallon-size Ziploc bag from her. It held little Eli's shorts, Tshirt, underpants, and tennis shoes. That was a long time ago. Travis is a fine young man, happily married, with two sweet children of his own, Madalyn and Mason. Even though it was a long time ago, I am weeping as I write this. It still hurts so much. I loved that little boy, and my heart hurt for his parents and his brother. My tears were and are like those Jesus shed outside Lazarus's tomb. His tears were for the pain in the hearts of Mary and Martha, His dear friends, even though Jesus knew in just moments He would by His mighty power bring Lazarus back to life. I knew then that Eli was alive and in the arms of Jesus. There has never been any doubt.

Just a few summers ago, Jared's mama contacted me to say she and Jared wanted to invite me to come see Jared baptized. He was twelve years old at that time. The baptism would be in the New River, and she gave me directions to the place and told me to wear tennis shoes to walk through the grass and weeds down to the river. I thanked her and said I'd be there. It was so amazing to see Jared baptized in the river. It filled my heart to overflowing to see with my own eyes and think of Jesus's baptism in the Jordan River. I know God has great things in store for Jared.

When my own children were little, they wore undershirts (a T-shirt under their outer shirt) to keep them warm in wintertime. That only lasted a few years when other mamas were dressing their children that way. Just a few years back, we had a tiny little boy named Michael in our class. He was such a cute little blond. One very cold winter morning, he came to school wearing a sweatshirt with the bottom band so stretched out that it stood away from his small body. He came up to Mrs. Liddle and said, "I'm told [cold], Mrs. Liddle." She went to get a large-size blanket that we had in our classroom.

She wrapped it around Michael and lifted him up on her lap, cuddling her arms around him. Michael's great-grandpa brought him to school every day. He had told us that both Michael's parents were in prison for drugs. Just a few days later, Michael went to Mrs. Liddle, saying, "I'm told adin [I'm cold again]." She got the blanket and held and cuddled that sweet child. How our hearts hurt for this dear little boy and other children like him, who had been robbed of love and affection by parents who made the wrong choices for their lives and his. God kept my path crossing with Michael's great-grandpa's every few months so I could ask about Michael. Michael has gone to live in Maryland with his grandma, and he was very happy there.

Kenny lived right next door to the church with two people who were his grandparents though he called them Mama and Papa. His parents were in prison for drugs. Mike and Louise loved Kenny, and we all became friends during the two years he was in nursery school, as a three-year-old and a four-year-old. Louise had lung cancer and had to go to Winston-Salem (one-and-a-quarter-hour trip) for chemo once a week. When Mike told me this at school, he said, "Kenny will have to miss school on Thursdays because we can't get back in time to pick him up."

I said, "If you and Louise want, I'd be glad to take Kenny home with me for lunch. We could play at my house, and you could pick him up when you get back."

Mike said, "That would be great! Thank you."

So I told Mike to bring a change of play clothes to keep at my house. There was a creek in my backyard, just deep enough to cover your feet and wide enough to step across. Of course, little boy and creek = wet clothes. So Kenny went home with me on Thursdays. He would go into my son Chris's bedroom to change into his play clothes while I fixed lunch. Chris was living in Blacksburg while attending Virginia Tech. A few weeks later, Mike called from the hospital in Winston-Salem to say that Louise had a bad reaction to the chemo, and the doctor had admitted her to stay overnight. I said Kenny could stay with me until they returned the next day. Mike told me where a key was hidden outside their home so Kenny and I could go in and get his pj's and toothbrush.

Kenny stayed and was quite content. We said prayers at bedtime. All along Kenny had heard me pray at lunch, thanking God for food to eat, the creek to play in and the yard, for nursery school, and all our friends and family. The next day Mike came to pick up Kenny after he got Louise settled at home. After that, Kenny called Chris's room *his* room. I teased Chris about it. Early in December that year, I asked Mike and Louise if I could pick up Kenny to go to Sunday school and church. They said yes. I took paper, pen, and crayons to worship, and Kenny and I drew and colored during the sermon. We drew Christmas trees, houses, churches, the manger holding baby Jesus, Mary, Joseph, an angel, three camels, three gifts, a huge star, and birthday cake. My church has a big, beautiful Christmas performance every year. I invited Mike and Louise, even though they did not attend any church. They came and brought Kenny. All the rest of that school year, the summer months, and the next school year, Kenny went to Sunday school and church with me. During that winter, Louise died. A few years later on, Mike fell in love and married a nice lady. She not only loved Mike, she loved Kenny too. I was invited and joyfully attended their wedding. It was held in the lady's backyard. They were happy together, the three of them for many years. There will always be a special place in my heart for Kenny.

One year a very long time ago, we had three children's families with one parent battling cancer. One daddy and two mamas. We teachers sought to encourage their families with words of comfort. We prayed fervently for all of them. Some of the other children's families knew what was happening. Somehow we knew that the end of our school year could not be the last time we'd all be together. We teachers talked it over and decided that we would have a pot-luck picnic two weeks after our last day, at Felts Park (our city's park). Our park has a large covered area with picnic tables and barbecue area and swings, jungle gym, sandbox pits, and a grassy area for Frisbees and Hula-Hoops. God gave us an absolutely beautiful evening, and everyone was so happy to see each other. We had lots of wonderful food, and the children ran and played and had so much fun! Lindsey's daddy and Zackery's mama both died a few months later. Jillian's mama is alive and well today. I occasionally see Lindsey, Zackery, and Jillian's mama. Both Lindsey and Zackery are married now.

Every once in a great while, I see Colt's mama, who still lives in the area. When Colt was in my four-year class, a terrible accident happened at his home. Colt found a loaded gun and accidentally shot his younger sister in the head. His sister was rushed to the hospital. She did not die but was in the hospital a long time and had permanent damage. Everyone in our small town knew what had happened. Colt's mama called me, saying, "I'm sure you know about Colt accidentally shooting his sister, and you probably don't want him to come back to nursery school." I said, "Of course we want Colt to come back. He's more than welcome here. How is Cherisa, and how are you?" We talked. I told her that the other teachers and I had been praying for them. Colt returned.

You know how it hurts when you hit your funny bone? Well, one little dark-haired beauty named Rachel banged her elbow on the corner of a table as she was hurrying by. She turned quickly to me and said, "O-o-oh, I hurt my bell-bow."

Rachel's daddy was my pastor at First Baptist Church, in Galax, Virginia. Our classroom and door were decorated for Valentine's Day. We had a Snoopy poster with Snoopy in front of his doghouse, and the sign on his doghouse read "Kisses $1." Above the doghouse, a banner read, "The Fabulous Kisser Is In." As Rachel came smiling into our room, her daddy pointed to the poster and asked, "Which one is the Fabulous Kisser?" And Carol and I, just like two children would do, quickly pointed to each other. He laughed, and so did we. And every year when we decorate for Valentine's, I remember.

One time, more than thirty-five years ago, someone asked me, "How much money do you make at nursery school?" And I answered "Oh, about $1.98 an hour and all the hugs and kisses you can get in three hours."

I wish parents and grandparents really know how important their words are. Words not only enter a child's ears but their hearts as well. Words should encourage, praise, comfort, heal, and help. Your words, building up or tearing down, which will you choose?

When parents separate or one parents dies, the child is the one who loses the most. But adults get so caught up in what they want and how they feel that they are blinded to the needs of the child. The most innocent one, the most vulnerable one, is the one who pays the biggest price. Not just for a few days or months, but all their lives. I know there are times when one parent fails to be a good parent, and the other parent is left alone with the child or children to raise. One little boy said one morning, "My mama's in jail. She kicked our door down last night." She had been on drugs. I later learned that she had literally kicked their door down. A few years later, the daddy remarried, a fine young woman I'd known for several years. They had dated for a long time, while she was building a friendship with him and his two sons, Luke and his older brother. The older brother competed in national rodeos. They are a happy family today.

Another day a child said, "Today my daddy's in jail."

"I'm sorry," I told the child. Then I said, "I've got the Hungry Hippos game in our cabinet. Let's go get it, and you and a friend can play it. I'll show you how to play it."

Music was always a huge part of our nursery school days. Singing lifts the heart to a happier place. So many grown-ups never know that or have long since forgotten it. We sang "Where Is Thumbkin?" and "If You're Happy and You Know It." You should recognize and remember these and, of course, "Jesus Loves Me." We sang "The Leaves Are Falling Down" in the fall and "Snowflakes Are Falling" in winter. We sang "Six White Ducks" and "Birdie Birdie, Where Is Your Nest?" in spring. We sang many other songs, and they all had hand motions. Sometimes we were standing and moving while singing. But the all-time favorite was "The Skunk Song." The children enjoyed the story *Skunks! Go to Bed!* in the winter, and we learned the song that day. In the story, three skunks, Willy, Wally, and Lulu (brothers and sister) didn't want to go to bed. Sound familiar to you parents of young children? The other animals in the forest wanted to hibernate. So they had to figure out a way to put those three skunks to sleep. The words and motions to the "Skunk Song" are as follows:

> I stuck my head in a little skunk's hole. (Make circle with your hands, not touching, and stick head in while singing or saying words.)
>
> The little skunk said, "Well, bless my soul!" (Look surprised and gently smack your hand to the side of your face.)
>
> Take it out, take it out, take it out, *remove it*! (Speak kindly on each "Take it out," but louder and more firmly on "*Remove it!*" Point thumb sideways each time while saying "Take it out," using one thumb then the other one. Both hands

palms down cross each other vigorously while saying "*Remove it!*")

Well, I didn't remove it like the little skunk said. (Shake your head while saying the words.)

If you don't remove it, you'll wish you had! (Pointing and shaking your finger strongly.) He turned around, he raised his tail, he went "Pssssh!" (Turn around, raise one arm with your hand curved, shaking it as you say "Pssssh!")

I removed it. (Say slowly after pinching both sides of your nose together.)

God gave me the words and tune to two songs that we taught the children. We sang on the way to the playground and back. "Thank you, God, for a sunshiney day, a sunshiney day, a sunshiney day. Thank you, God, for a sunshiney day, so I can go out to play." The other song God gave me later one night during the time we were in our alphabet study. The words and motions are as follows:

First verse:
God made the animals that we see. (Point to heaven, first two fingers point out, others and thumb closed together, move two fingers in front of eyes, sweeping left to right.)

The birds in the air and the fish in the sea. (One hand makes fluttering motion overhead, then one hand makes swimming motion down in front of child's body.)

God gave the animals just what they need. (Point to heaven and nod head.)

Their home, and their food, and their family. (Hold one hand up in front with fingers and thumb closed inside, lift one finger, and tap gently with pointer finger from other hand for *home, food, family*.)

Second verse:
>   God made the animals that we see. (Repeat motions from first verse.)
>   The birds in the air and the fish in the sea.
>   God made the animals and you and me! (Point to others, point to self.)
>   God loves the animals and you and me! (Point to heaven, then cross arms over heart and press like a hug. Point to child and self while smiling.)

How could you not smile when you think about it? He did give you your home, your food, and your family. You are thinking, "Oh, no, I bought my home or built my home or I'm paying for my home." But think one minute, who gave you a good mind and a strong body so you can work, earn money, and buy a home. The same is true for your food, whether you grow it, can it, freeze it, or buy it. It all comes from God's gracious hand to bless you. And your family, your husband or wife, your child or children, are all a gift for you to make you happy and to teach you many things. If you never knew it before, you can learn what real love is. It is always putting her or him or them first, no matter what it costs you. And doing that without wanting praise or favors in return will become a sweet reward for you. It truly is more blessed to give than to receive.

We sang at Thanksgiving "There Are Many Things I Am Thankful For." This was both a song and a game. At one point, the teachers would touch a child's head, and he or she was to very quickly name something or someone. At Christmas, we sang "Jingle Bells," "Up on the Housetop," "Joy to the World," and "Follow the Star." At Valentine's, we sang "Love Somebody," "Yes, I Do," "Oh, Valentine!" and "Jesus Loves Me." At party day, we taught the daddies "Oh, Valentine!" so if this year or any year he goes home on Valentine's Day with no flowers, no candy, and no card, he can simply sing this little song. *Guaranteed*, she'll love it. Here are the words and motions

Oh, Valentine. Oh Valentine.

Oh, will you be my Valentine? (When saying "Valentine," draw a huge heart in the air in front of you using pointer fingers, drawing both sides of heart at once. Saying "you," point to her. Saying "my," point to yourself and repeat.)

At Easter we sang "Oh, How He Loves You and Me," "I've Got the Joy, Joy, Joy, Joy Down in My Heart" (other verses, "Love of Jesus" and "Peace that Passeth Understanding,") also "Peace Like a River." The children really loved singing these last two with not just hand motions but whole body. (Clap hands loudly on each "Joy, joy"; point finger right hand as if going down into the heart each time; hug yourself and move body side to side during "Love of Jesus;" during Passeth, move your hands palms open, gently smacking while passing.)

Second song, "Peace Like a River," both hands start flowing slowly as far left as you can reach, while seated, with fingers wiggling go as far right. Then repeat. While singing "In my soul," place one hand over heart and the other on top of it. For "Joy Like a Fountain," hop up with fingers wiggling in front of you up as high as you can reach, then wiggling down the sides like water in a fountain. "Love Like an Ocean," while seated, move both arms to far left, make big wave as arms reach center, then wave descends to the right and down.

During all these forty-two years with amazing children, there were some who were named Summer and Autumn, for God's seasons; Rose, Jasmyn and Lily for God's flowers; April and August for the months in the year; and Matthew, Mark, Luke and John, Malachi, Micah, Timothy, Samuel, Jeremiah, Daniel, Jonah, and Amos, all for the books of the Bible.

Laura and Lila were both so shy and wouldn't talk to anyone at first. But finally, Laura talked to me when she needed to go potty. She never talked to the children or the other teacher. Lila, after many weeks, began to talk to another girl.

Anthony had kidney disease, and Alexis had an insulin pump attached to her small body.

Simon had an EpiPen. God bless them and their families.

We had Sterling, Jade, Ebony, Ray, Bishop, Vincent, Sheena, Shawna, Braxton, Noelle, Scott, Fred, Victoria, Grant, Kyle, and Paul.

Addie had long, thick curly hair and had pretty bows in it every day. Azarea (pronounce it like "a-star-ree-uh") was her mama's precious little girl. Both Mama and Azarea were dressed beautifully every day, like they were models for TV commercials. But we teachers soon found out Mama was so kind-hearted.

Mary and Kelly are serving as missionaries. Kelly is in Czechoslovakia and has been for many years. Mary and her husband and their three children are in Turkey. They also have served the Lord for many years.

I pray for all the children down through the years and extra for Jay, a state trooper, as well as Jacob, Corey, and Drew on our local police department, and Graham, a professional firefighter.

It has been my joy and privilege to teach Andrew and Faith, two of my own dear grandchildren. I have taught nieces, Hayley, Brittany, Madison, and Carly. The nephews were Gray, Chas, Christian, Jack, and Austin. The children and grandchildren of my dear friends who also taught at nursery school were Margaret, Fred, Jada, Lindsey, Gayle, Sadie, Joshua, Jacob, Cole, Cody, Josh, Jordan, Zachary, Spenser, Patrick, Heather, Megan, Erin, Ellie, Kristin, Ethan, and Justin. You see, my family is huge! All the ladies who have worked here in the nursery school have been such a wonderful blessing to the children, all the members of their families, to each other, and to me. We all became like family. We felt like sisters. But I felt like Mama too! Because I was older and had walked much further down life's path. I had hired them and trained them. The only one that was hard to hire was Tracy. She was so sweet and such a good mama. But I was unsure of hiring her, because I didn't want to say or do anything that would hurt our friendship. I had been her Sunday school teacher for three years when she was in eighth, ninth, and tenth grade. God tied our heartstrings together then. You see, Tracy's daddy had been raising her and her sister by himself for many years. Tracy's dad was our city manager and completely devoted himself to raising those two girls, who were very young. I did hire Tracy, and we worked together for many years. She has been my daughter, the one I didn't give birth to.

In different classes, there was Blayze, freckle-faced, happy-natured, never in a hurry, and Steele, with perfect posture and determination. Mia, a dark-haired beauty who plans to swim in the Olympics in 2024. She's been on our swim team, competing and placing, since she was four. I remember Karlie always wanting "to help the teachers." So sweet!

Most Mamas do all they can to give their children every opportunity to do and be all they can. One extra special mama was Susan, whose three children, Tate, Jack, and Sophie, all came to nursery school. Both Tate and Sophie were born with cystic fibrosis, but not Jack. Their parents did not coddle Tate and Sophie. They helped them love life and be as fit and healthy as they could be. Not only did they take swimming lessons, but also became competitors on our city's swim team with their brother Jack. All three were active in scouting. Sophie won a food competition, and the prize was a trip to the White House to meet Michelle Obama. Our local newspaper featured a picture of Sophie, her mama, and Mrs. Obama along with a lengthy description of Sophie's adventure. Tate and Jack were in Boy Scouts. Tate has become an Eagle Scout, quite an accomplishment for any young man. I felt so blessed to be there at the ceremony.

One morning while we three teachers were helping children put on shirts over their clothes to protect clothes while they painted on easels. The three double-sided easels were set up at one end of our very large room. The huge wooden toy box with three shelves inside was at the other end of our room. That toy box held so much: milk crate full of pots, pans, dishes, etc.; a tub that held play food; a large wooden box on casters (to roll) filled with Lincoln Logs; tool boxes complete with tools; barrel of monkeys; tub of large colorful wooden beads for stringing together; Fisher-Price barn with cow, horse, pig, rooster, hen, sheep, dog, tractor, and wagon; large silo with lid; several pieces of fence that would stand up, a water trough, and a farmer. There was also a Fisher-Price house that opened apart, revealing upstairs and downstairs rooms. There were beds, table and chairs, a sofa, and of course a car for the garage. There were play people. We had the FisherPrice schoolhouse with a ringing school bell housed on the rooftop. One side of the roof flipped up and the side wall laid down. Inside were desks, a teacher, table and playground pieces—swings, a merry-go-round, and slide. There was a large bin of wooden blocks (natural color) and another bin of brightly painted blocks (red, green, yellow, blue, and orange). Three darling little boys played together every day. They were such good little boys to each other and the rest of the children. Their names were Jamar, Drew, and Jeremiah. They came up with a new idea while playing. They unloaded the toy box completely and quietly and then each climbed into a shelf as if they were in bunk beds. What a sight!

Two little boys named Trevor and John were in one of the earliest classes, probably year 3 or 4 in the 1970s. We had a book and puzzle shelf in our room. It held several books and about fifteen puzzles that related to the season and/or holiday we were learning about. The class had been told they could choose a book or puzzle and take it to the table nearby. When they finished, they should take it back to the shelf. If they couldn't work the puzzle, ask and one of us would help them. They could work as many puzzles as they wanted or look at as many books as they chose, one at a time. Well, just near the first month of school, John and Trevor began dumping many puzzles together on the tabletop. After talking to both boys, Carol and I wrote in our lesson plans, "*Remind Trevor and John—no puzzle-dumping!*" We had helped them to put all those puzzles back together. Here's a hint for parents today: explain why you did not like their behavior, what it cost. We told those boys if they and other children kept dumping puzzles, we'd run out of time to go outside to the playground near the end of the morning. We have to help children see why. Why they should listen and obey. Lesson: everyone's happier. But as parents, grandparents, and teachers, we have to explain the rules and remind and correct them and help them clean up the mess—and keep reminding. And very important, praise them for all good behavior, every kindness they show to anyone.

If you will be choosing a name for a child, let me share some of the names of my dear little ones. This list will not include every name, and they are not in any special order. There are comments on some, but not all. Abram, Geoffrey, Britt (mischievous); Kassie, Mandy, Stefan, Phillip, Shaina, Holly Beth, Bronson, Liam, Laci, Rachel Victoria, Wyndom, Noelle; Chevelle (shy) and Zoe (outspoken)—both wore glasses and were made solid as a rock; McCall, Caci, Natalie—headful of beautiful curls, so shy but blossomed! AJ—what a grin! He stole your heart. Angel, Tiarra, Brooke, Allie, Erin Elise, Stuart, Hadassah, Zeth, Robert, Sheridan, Rusty, Alyssa (a pint-sized cowgirl with platinum-blond hair); Sally—died with her mama in a car accident caused by a drunk driver; Dad became Catholic priest after that. Savannah—dressed up like a princess every day. Maleke—gentle, kind to everyone, loads of soft big curls on his head, chocolate brown. Malachi—small, so serious till you finally reached his heart. Maiya, Brogan, Zarah, Sam, Laken, Karisma, Crockett, Chip, Chantel—so quiet, soft smile, and shy. Cullen—warmed your heart with his smile when he came in the door. Jeremy—tiny magician brought two tricks to school to show his friends. I pray he has found magic to be empty, an illusion, and that he has found Jesus, the truth, the way, and the life. Stanley—studying to be a doctor. Derek—clogging at Tweetsie Railroad, Boone, North Carolina. Paige—wanted to water the plants every morning. Cheyanne and Bailey—didn't know each other before nursery school, but became best friends, played together every day, and then with Disney's Frozen, they played and sang it, so did Jack.

Aiden—only child, only wanted to play but really didn't know how to play with others, until he became interested in playing with Bailey and Cheyanne. Julian—smart, gifted with a loving Christian mama and a father, a devoted Muslim. Dane, Reed, Weston, Crue.

When I hear the word *rodeo*, I immediately think of Shawn, who said he wanted to be a bull rider when he grew up. And years later, there was Molly, who did become a barrel racer in rodeos.

George—wore glasses and always wore a serious expression. Fred—also serious but knew how to laugh and enjoy being with other children, so smart, distinctive voice. Amber, Ebony, Parker, Marisa, Collin—perfect posture, Dad was in the military. Collin learned to have fun at school. Patrice—pretty and sweet little black girl who grew up to become a model and then design clothes. Sarah is in the program to become an astronaut for NASA. Kristen is at Harvard, soon to graduate with a law degree. Matthew served in a nuclear submarine under the polar ice cap. Heather, Mallie, Patrick—freckles, sweet smile. Scarlett was so obviously loved by her daddy. She just lit up when she saw him, and his reaction was double hers. He was a long-distance truck driver, probably six feet, four or five inches. He looked like he could play linebacker in the NFL, but we teachers saw he was a giant marshmallow inside.

Two separate years the children in our classes were given a special treat, to make and decorate their own gingerbread house to take home that morning. The first time this was done by a child's mama, and the next time, years later, by a grandma and her daughter for her son. The daughter had also been in our class years ago. Both times these sweet ladies not only furnished everything needed but had a small piece of cardboard covered with Reynold's Wrap and the house (graham crackers held together with stiff icing) ready. They had brought gumdrops, M&M's (yes, a few got eaten!), sprinkles, candy canes, pretzels (straight for walk and curved for fences), gummy bears and trees for the yard. They had sandwich baggies with the icing inside and one corner snipped off for squirting. Three children decorated theirs, while three others watched and waited for their turn. You see, it is part of every parent, grandparent, and teacher's job to teach children how to wait. To wait patiently and enjoy the watching and waiting for the good thing to come. Not fussing or whining or demanding their way. If only adults knew that taking time to tell children what is ahead helps them behave. Before we began to make the gingerbread houses, we told the children in our classroom that everyone would get to make one today and decorate it and take it home today. Then one teacher took three children to the room next door to make their gingerbread house and three others to watch. They would be next. Everyone was happy and excited. We had small slips of paper with the children's names printed to be scotch-taped down on the edge of the cardboard base. Thanks, Charlotte, Cherie, and Corey!

About waiting, talk to your child every night before you listen to their prayers. Tell them something good they did or said that day. If you didn't see anything, tell them, "I'm so glad you are my sweet little girl [or boy]." If they weren't sweet that day, just say, "I love you. You are my precious child." Then you pray out loud. Thank God for the day, that we are well and live where we are warm. Thank Him for food. Thank Him for your child and/or children. Call them by name. Their names and yours God has written in the palms of His hands. In the palms of Jesus's hands are the nail scars left when He paid for the sins of all people for all time. Take time! It doesn't matter what is on TV, the Super Bowl or the last game of the World Series or the Indy 500. How you handle bedtime for your child is crucial for their future. Don't fumble this, or strike out, or hit the wall.

For several years, our classes visited the dairy farm of a nursery school daddy. We went through a room that held the huge refrigerated tank where the milk was stored until the refrigerated truck came to pick it up. The dairy farmer had hand-written a Bible verse with magic marker on a sheet of paper and taped it on the milk-holding tank, where you'd see it when you came in the door. He told me that he changed the verse daily. Then he led us, teachers and children, into the milking area. He told us the cows had to be milked twice every day. He showed us the milking apparatus and let the children feel the suction as he held it against the palms of their hands. Then the cows came in. Their teats were sanitized, and the milkers were attached. We could see white milk going through the hose and on its way through clear tubes to the huge storage tank. The children were fascinated. One child asked, "Which one gives chocolate milk?" The farmer laughed and said, "The cows only give white milk, and later people add chocolate to it." Next the farmer told us we were going outside to feed the baby calves with big baby bottles. He said, "You'll have to hold on tight because they will suck hard." The calves were each in what looked like large doghouses. They were chained so they couldn't get out. Two children together held a bottle for a calf, all the way down the row. You never heard so many squeals and happy giggles coming from our children. Before leaving, we sang a song for the dairy farmer.

> Thank you, cows, for the milk we drink. (One hand holds pretend glass, the other pours milk into it while we sing and pretend to drink it.)
> Milk we drink. (Repeat motions.) Milk we drink. (Repeat motions.)
> We say moo! to you. (Cup hands on cheeks.)
> Thank you, cows, for the sweet ice cream. (Hold pretend ice cream cone and lick it.)
> Sweet ice cream. (Repeat motions.)

Sweet ice cream. (Repeat motions.)
We say "Yum! Yum! Yum!" (Rub your hands
in circles around your tummy.)

The children in our four-year-old classes learned about the life of George Washington and Abraham Lincoln and what was happening in our country when they were elected. They learned that these two men were opposites in their childhood, George Washington's family was wealthy. Abraham Lincoln's family was one of modest means, but both were great presidents. Each one struggled through a war here in America. We said we live in the greatest country in the world.

The children learned that Washington and Lincoln loved God, read His Bible, and prayed for help. The children learned about slavery and how black families were pulled apart as Daddy was sold to one farmer and his wife and children to another far away. They learned that President Lincoln visited the injured soldiers in the hospital. We showed them pictures of both President George Washington, the Washington Monument, President Abraham Lincoln, the Lincoln Memorial, and the money that bears their image (bills and coins). They learned about Lincoln's assassination and that the Civil War ended. The slaves were freed. We learned about our country's flag. In America, we are free to live, work, and worship God. God has richly blessed America. George Washington was the general leading the soldiers, fighting right with them to keep us free. After the war, his men said he was first in war, first in peace, and first in the hearts of his countrymen. He was elected the first president. Abraham Lincoln, nicknamed Honest Abe, was the president during another time of war in our country. Each of them, Washington and Lincoln, was known for his honesty and his love for all Americans.

There were many families that we had their only child or some of their children or both of their children. There were three families who each had three children that we so looked forward to having number 3. Because we had loved the older children and grew to love and respect the parents. The first family came many years ago. On get-acquainted meeting night, the children and parents were there. As people left, one set of parents began helping us teachers pick up and put away the many toys we'd had out for the children to play. We said, "Oh, you don't have to help us." The daddy spoke up, smiling, "Oh, we are glad to help you all." I had heard this before from many mamas but never a daddy and a mama, as she quickly agreed. Smith and Emily, you helped too. No wonder we teachers looked forward to having Isaiah and having contact with that special family again.

The second wonderful family had Andrew, Ashley, and Joey (faster than a speeding bullet!). Jimmy, the daddy, absolutely absorbed himself in being Daddy. He was and is 50 percent little boy and 50 percent clown inside a grown man. He came often, bringing his children to school and picking them up. For many years, he would show up, unannounced, bringing a "magic coloring book" from Ringling Brothers Circus. He would then entertain the class, showing them the bright colored circus scenes and ask them to help him do magic. They were to think hard to make the pictures disappear. Then after he counted to three, everyone would blow hard. He'd open the book, flipping the blank pages. Next, he'd ask the class to bring the bright colored pages back by the same magic trick again. They loved it!

The third dear family had Evan, with a smile that seemed to go all around his head. Lena, his sister, a petite dark-haired beauty who just hugged and hugged you every day. How sweet that was! Once again we teachers could hardly wait for baby Nicholas to get big enough to come to us. He finally did. At our end-of-the-year picnic, Dad came to me, saying, "Thank you all for the many good things you've taught our children," as he handed me a check—a love gift. I said, "It has been a joy!"

While I've mentioned the daddies of these three families, I know how important you mamas have been—Marcie, Angela, and Sendella. A mama ties the heartstrings of the family.

Three of my little boys, Timothy, Hunter, and Justin, lead worship services now. And Jake (remember the little Superman?) is the choir director of a large church. That brings a smile to my face.

Hunter works at Subway, where I eat lunch. He brought his phone to me so I could see him and hear the message he delivered at his church last Sunday. It was wonderful, and my tears of joy flowed. I told him I was so proud of him.

Isaac had a good chance for a career in baseball. An injury changed that, but now he is selling real estate in Myrtle Beach, South Carolina, and happily married.

Other names of dear children were the following:

Kelsey—sweetheart with a beautiful smile, will be a nurse. Gracie—so smart and cute (her mama had been in my class at age four and is now my dentist). J. Luke—loved school and all his classmates. Irelyn—a slender beauty with platinum-blond hair and kindness for everyone.

Sydney—got a hairline crack in her thumb's bone from lurching forward as she climbed down on the playground's rope net. She'd been accidentally bumped by another child who was nearby. Steven—a cute little black boy, while riding a stick horse, accidentally knocked over blocks another child was playing with. He heard it, turned around and saw, and said, "A man's gotta do what a man's gotta do." Then he lay down his horse and began helping to rebuild. (Good lesson here: even if you didn't mean to break something, stop and help make things right.) Stacey—short, big brown eyes, deep voice. Sherri, Mazie, Ruston, Laiken, Missy, Robin, Kolby, Allen, Caylin, Josh, Claudia—sweet child whose grandma was Native American.

Kasey—a ray of sunshine every day with her bouncy head of curls and a big smile. Marleigh—should be in the Miss America pageant when she grows up. Samantha, Jessie, Louis (pronounced Loo-ee), Hollan—so blessed to have her grandma, Bitha, her daddy, and grandpa to raise her and her brothers. JJ—so sweet and so fortunate to be adopted into his loving family, parents and grandparents. Brian—stubborn, Bryan—meek. They come both ways, you know. You help meek feel more able to succeed. You help stubborn begin to see sometimes you're right, sometimes you're not, and sometimes you can, sometimes you cannot. Both boys came to a better place.

There is a miniature horse farm located a few miles from our city limits. I knew the lady and her husband who owned it. They had a herd of about 150 miniature horses. People from all over the United States bought horses there. So one day I thought our four-year-old class would love seeing the horses. So I went to their house unannounced and talked with Mr. and Mrs. Kegley about my class and asked if we could come to visit. I assured them the children would be very well-behaved. We would prepare them before we came, explaining no yelling (that would scare the horses, and they would run away) and no climbing on the wooden slatted fence. We wouldn't want to break the fence, because the horses could get out and maybe get hit by a car or truck.

The Kegleys said no other class or children's group of any kind had ever come. I told them about our classes going year after year to visit at the library, radio station, the police department, a dentist's office, a dairy farm, and the fire department. Each time I called in advance to get permission and schedule a day and time. We were always welcomed back, and many said, "Your classes listen and behave better than older classes do." So the Kegleys said, "Yes, we'll try it just this once, and no other groups will be allowed here." I thanked them. We set a day and time.

Mrs. Kegley said, "The local bread store will give you day-old light bread, several loaves free. The horses love it. They will eat it right from the children's hands." We set a date and time. We went. The children loved it! The horses were happy too. The children fol-lowed me to the Kegley's back patio area, where we made a large circle and said a huge thank you for letting us come. Then we sang a few of our springtime songs. Mr. and Mrs. Kegley loved it. Our class (the only one allowed) went year after year. Thank you, once again, Mrs. Kegley for allowing our children to have this special experience.

Another amazing horse experience, years later on, came to me. My friend Pam Harris is also my pharmacist. She knew I worked at the nursery school and one day said, "I have a beautiful white Arabian mare that I've taken to show children's groups before. Would you like me to bring her for your class to see there at the church out in the yard?"

"Oh yes, that would be great!" I answered.

Then Pam said, "I'll bring treats for Beloved and help the children feed them to her. I'll bring bright-colored finger paint and pans for it. So the children can choose a color for each hand and place their hands on Beloved's side, leaving their handprints. I'll have wet wipes and paper towels for the children to clean up. After the whole class has had a turn, they can all have another turn to give Beloved a treat and do handprints again with different colors. We'll lift them up to reach her back and neck." Of course, I had told the class earlier about Beloved and Pam the day they came. I showed the children, using one to demonstrate. "You put one hand behind your back and keep it there while giving Beloved a treat. Your other hand will be flat, fingers straight, palm up. A teacher or Ms. Pam will hold your fingers and thumb down. The treat goes on your palm, and Beloved will use her lips to gobble it up. It will tickle you, but it will not hurt. After you give Beloved her treat, you may pet her if you want to. You don't have to."

By the time all the boys and girls had done the second treat, they all wanted to pet Beloved. Not only did my friend Pam furnish everything needed for this once-in-a-lifetime experience, but she made pictures of the children standing in front of the beautifully painted horse and later gave me a copy for every child to keep. She also gave horse coloring books to every child. Ms. Pam and Beloved came to visit an two days back-to-back, so both of my classes of four-year-olds could enjoy it. Now that all seems like a huge gift to all of us at nursery school, and it was. But that was not all Pam did. She also bathed Beloved the day before their visit, the afternoon after the first visit, and then again after the second day visit. That's right, three baths for Beloved and lots of work for Pam. I can never thank this lady enough. If there was a gold medal for blessing children, Pam, you would win one, hands down. (Pardon the pun.)

One year on our way back to the church from our class's visit to Kegley's miniature horse farm, we passed McDonald's, and I saw elephants in the parking lot. They were not close to the highway but closer to the back of McDonald's. The other teacher in the van did not see them, so I'm sure she wondered when I said, "I'm going to turn us around and go back because I saw elephants in the parking lot at McDonald's." Sure enough, there they were! Three Indian elephants securely chained to weighted heavy drums eating from large hay bales. I parked the van and got out to ask if our class could get out and watch. He said yes. I got back in the van and talked with the other teacher, and then we told the children where we'd stand and remember quiet voices. One child spoke up, saying, "Loud scares animals."

"Very good remembering," I answered.

Then we got out, made a curved line, and watched. I asked the children, "Are these elephants African or Indian?"

"Indian," they answered.

"How did they know?" the man asked.

A child spoke up, "Because their ears are not huge."

Another child said, "Elephants in Africa have really big ears so they can fan themselves like this to get cool." He put his arms up the sides of his head and moved them back and forth.

The man was amazed. He asked how old the children were. We said four or five. He said, "They are really smart." Yes, they were. They were the only class to ever see the elephants near McDonald's, but every class learned about elephants, where God put them in the world, what they ate, what their babies were called, how they protected themselves, the name of a group of them and their enemies. After that, we loaded up in the van and returned to the church.

Some other children who came to nursery school were as follows: Shannon, Bradley, Cassidy, Ryan, Madelyn, Lura, Hayden, Forrest, Teresa, Coy, Ava, Coleman, Hylie, Colson, Brooke, Kimberly, Audrey, Carrie Sage, Courtney, Aisha, Tabitha, Leigh Anne, Tanner, Taylor, Marianne, Jill, Julie, Rebecca, Lovina, Owen, Talisha, Alicia, Alec, and Alex.

Probably twenty-five years ago, I got a phone call from a mama whose little girl, Caitlin, was in the fourth grade that year. Her child's teacher had announced that they would be having a special day in just two weeks. It would be a day when every child's Grandma could visit the class. After each boy and girl introduced their grandma, the class would give cards they had hand-made to the grandmas, and then they would enjoy refreshments together. Caitlin's mama explained that her grandmas lived too far away to come. Caitlin had said to her mama, "I wish Mrs. Hennis could come and be my grandma for that day." So Caitlin's mama talked to her teacher. She approved. I went and felt so honored and loved to be there with Caitlin. I still have a picture of the two of us her Mama made that day. Remember, love never ends. That's one of God's promises. He is faithful to keep all his promises.

Unusual names: Bentley, Whatley, and Smoky. Why would anyone choose to name a pretty little girl Bentley or Whatley? I could never figure those out, and then years later a grandma called to get her little four-year-old grandson in our class. She said his name was Smoky. We planned to meet at the school so she could fill out the forms. I asked her to bring his original birth certificate, not a copy. I had to see the original, check the child's name, both parents' names, and feel the state seal, as required by law. She came and was filling out our forms, while I was checking his birth certificate. You probably won't believe this, but his first and middle names were Smoky Bear. Then, astonished, I said, "His real name is Smoky Bear?"

"Oh, yes," she replied, "I don't know what my son was thinking." So we called him Smoky—poor child.

During our country's last census, I was working as a census-taker far out in the county. I had street or road names and house numbers on my paperwork. And I was surprised when one of my nursery school mamas answered the door. She was surprised too. After hellos, I asked about her two sons who had been in my class many years ago. She said, "Caleb's here now, home from college." She called his name, and in just a minute he walked into the room. She said, "Do you remember Mrs. Hennis from nursery school?"

"Sure," Caleb answered. "I haven't seen you in a long time."

Then as I asked about his life, he told me about college and how the previous summer he'd gone on a mission trip and done some building. Caleb told me it had been so rewarding to help others and do it all to honor God. Immediately, I knew that I should tell him and his mama about a plan I had. Our winter weather here where I live lasts till mid-May each year. I had learned near the end of March that a neighbor of mine had a very large hole in the floor of a bedroom in her house. The person who told me said it was about three and a half feet across, and the ground showed underneath. I had gone to the government agency that does weatherization for low-income families and was told there was a long waiting list, and everyone had to go on the end of it. So I had a plan to get that fixed in June myself, when I'd get my first paycheck as a census worker. I asked Caleb if he'd like to meet me there to look at it, and if he chose to do the work, I would pay for materials and his time and hard work.

We met the next afternoon. I had visited my neighbor that morning and told her I wanted to see if I could get someone to fix her floor. When Caleb and I went to her house, we were both shocked to see that the floor had rotted away. Only about one foot of floor was attached to the walls. The room was probably sixteen square feet. It was a very old home and had not been built well. No subfloor, no insulation. Just floor built about two feet above the earth. Of course, both Caleb and I knew this job would be much bigger than we'd thought. Caleb took measurements. The poor lady had used large cardboard boxes, broken down and flattened out to cover the ground in an effort to keep out the cold. Both Caleb's and my heart broke for this lady. We hid our feelings and thanked her for letting us come. I told her I'd talk to her in a day or two.

I didn't know what plans Caleb had for his summer or even if he'd want to tackle this job alone. But God bless His sweet heart, Caleb said he'd do the figuring on materials he'd need to include subfloor, insulation, and floor. He'd check our building supply stores, get figures, and call me the next day. I reminded him I would pay for all materials and his time and labor. Caleb worked really hard and did a fine job. We were both so happy when it was finished. So was the lady. She thanked us with tears in her eyes. I paid for the materials, but Caleb would not take a penny for his time and hard work! He said he enjoyed working for God. I know God has richly repaid Caleb, and someday I'll see him get his heavenly reward. I'll be smiling, and the tears of joy will be flowing down my face. Guess what, that lady only used that floor for two years, until Habitat for Humanity tore down her old house and built a new one for her—complete with all new appliances, furniture, curtains, dishes, pots and pans, the works. How wonderful!

For ten years, the two four-year-old classes at First United Methodist Church Nursery School in Galax, Virginia, rode in a trike-a-thon for St. Jude's Children's Research Hospital. Our trike-a-thon was a two-morning event. Our classes each had a maximum enrollment of twenty-five children with three teachers. Our school had a three-morning class and a two-morning class. While it took a lot of work by the teachers and a lot of work on the part of the children's families, who asked for donations from their friends, neighbors, coworkers, and family members, it was an absolutely wonderful experience for all of us. The children came to school the morning of the trike-a-thon so excited. A few days before, they had seen the video that St. Jude's had sent us. It showed other classes of boys and girls riding their bikes and trikes and having fun. It also showed children in St. Jude's with their families and the nurses and doctors. Children walking beside an IV pole, wearing a mask. Children in a hospital bed looking so tired and with no hair on their little heads.

A healthy child is such a wonderful blessing. This would be a good time to take a moment to praise God for your own child, children, grandchild, each one. We had talked with our classes, explaining that the children were sick, not an upset tummy or sore throat, but a different kind of sick that only happens to a few children. But the doctors and nurses and St. Jude's have a very strong medicine that helps boys and girls get well. The video also taught bike safety with Bikewell Bear and showed prizes the children could win for three levels of donations. The church had given us permission to rope off a part of the parking lot for the trike-a-thon. The children's families brought their trikes or bikes and helmets. The children came on in to school for a short playtime, during which we took a few at a time to go potty, until everyone had gone. Then the class sat in the semicircle of chairs while we explained we would all put our jackets on and walk in a nice line out to the parking lot. Our bikes or trikes would be in a line.

"The families will be out there to watch you. Please stay in the line until a teacher says, 'Go get on your trike and wait.' She will tell you which ones ride first. You'll go around a few times, until she says, 'One more time around, then park your trike and sit on it.' You listen and obey. Then the second group will ride going around a few times."

All along, the teachers and family members and the waiting children's group would be cheering for the riders. We repeated the whole process. After everyone was parked, we asked the children if they had ever seen the car races on TV. Several said yes. Then we said, "You were good drivers today. On the TV races, there is only one winner, and he takes a victory lap all by himself while everyone watches and cheers. Well today, all of you boys and girls are the winners, because our trike-a-thon is helping who?"

The class shouted, "Children at St. Jude's!"

"That's right, good for you. When you hear your name, ride around again. Because you are a winner." We called their names two or three at a time until every child was riding our victory lap. The families and teachers cheered loudly. What a wonderful time it was. During the ten years our nursery school did trike-a-thons, our total donations were $26,762.35. If you are a parent or grandparent I would like to encourage you to donate to St. Jude's for their birthday.

Early years at nursery school, we had a Halloween party, and the children could wear or bring their costume. It was fun for many years, but then things changed. One little boy came with his daddy through our door on party day dressed as Freddie Krueger. My heart almost stopped. He had the long sharp blades on all his fingers (of course, they were plastic) and what looked like blood splattered on the front of his white outfit. At that very moment, I knew we would never again have a Halloween party with children wearing costumes. I drafted a letter to the parents of that class. Here's a copy of that letter, sent more than twenty-five years ago. We continued to have parties, have fun stories, and do Halloween art and music and talk about safety.

Dear Parents,

I know you love your child and want what is best for them. This letter comes to you because of our love for your child and a growing concern for things that threaten them.

We encourage you to carefully consider that something as simple as helping your child choose a costume to wear at Halloween is important. Help your child by guiding him or her to select a positive character, one who helps others or is gentle. There is so much evil in our world today. We have all heard or seen on the news things we would never have believed could happen.

So many of the popular toys in recent times actually promote aggressive behavior in children. The Ninja Turtles and Power Rangers have a negative effect on children, both boys and girls. We do not allow the children at nursery school to play as these characters because that play involves

70

kicking and rough play. We do not allow children to pretend to shoot at each other. We cannot let them practice actions that could end in tragedy later, because we do love them.

When we were children, we lived in very different times than your children do today. We ran, played ball and hide 'n' seek and tag. We dressed up and pretended to be cowboys or play house. Today's children see murder nightly on TV. The world has changed so much since we were the children. It is harder today to keep children protected and innocent throughout childhood. They are exposed to so much that is harmful at a very early age. Through television, movies, and music, today's children are told and shown things that they are too young to see and hear. There are so few good role models for children and youth.

You, more than anyone else, will help mold and shape your child into the man or woman they will become. Don't miss any opportunity to fill your child's mind and heart with things that are good and pure and lovely.

With love,
the nursery school teachers

I remember a mama who dearly loved her three sons. The youngest two were twins, Eric and Ryan. Those two little boys constantly had the snottiest noses you would ever see. Every school day, their noses were full of yellow or greenish mucous. We would help them blow and blow to get all that mess out. Then we would take them to the bathroom, and we'd all wash hands. A lot of parents, down through the years, did not know that nasal mucous that is yellow or green means there is infection in the child's nasal cavities. One morning, as those twins and their mama came through the door, one boy sneezed. I quickly grabbed a tissue to help him, when Mama said, "I don't know why they both have such a mess in their noses."

I knew she smoked. I could smell it on her clothes. I said, "You smoke, don't you?"

"Yes," she answered, "but not in our house, I go outside."

"Do you smoke in your van?"

"Yes," she said. I told her I had grown up with two parents who smoked in the home and in the car. At a young age, I developed allergies because of that. Then I explained that the discolored mucous means infections. She said she didn't know that and thanked me for telling her. She said she was going to try to stop smoking. I said that would be a wonderful thing for her family and for her. Guess what? She did! And later told me she had. She was so glad! And so was I.

Here in Southwest Virginia, the dogwood trees bloom about the first week in May. Being our state flower, we taught the children about that beautiful blossom. It has four petals, two of those are slightly longer than the other two. That makes the shape of a cross. When you turn the bloom upside down, you will see all four petals appear to be notched and bloodstained. That reminds us of Jesus's hands and feet being nailed to the cross at Calvary, where He bled and died to save everyone who would believe in Him and ask Him to forgive them. Then when you turn the dogwood flower over again, you see the center, which reminds us of the crown of thorns the soldiers mockingly made and shoved down on His head.

At Easter, the children had learned many of the miracles Jesus had done—calming a fierce storm, feeding thousands with one little boy's lunch, healing a crippled man. They learned about the Last Supper, as Jesus did the job of a servant by washing the feet of his disciples. They learned how He and His friends went to the garden of Gethsemane to pray. How He was taken by the soldiers, the next day whipped until His back was bleeding. Then He carried His cross through Jerusalem and up the hill to Calvary. Then He lay down to pay the debt He did not owe. It was yours and mine. I told the children the words He said while He was on the cross and that He died and came back to life. He rose from the dead just as He had told His friends He would. And He *lives forever*. Then I told them God made the dogwood trees bloom every year just a few weeks after Easter to remind us all again that Jesus paid it all. Then we gave every child a dogwood blossom to take home that day, and I said, "Jesus wants you to tell your mama and daddy, your grandma and grandpa that Jesus loves them. Then you can show and tell them about the dogwood and how God makes it bloom every spring so we will all remember how much Jesus loves us."

One winter day shortly after I arrived at nursery school, the phone rang. It was Christopher's mother calling, saying her car wouldn't start and Christopher was crying. He wanted to come to school. I told her I'd come to get him if she wanted me to. She said, "Thank you. That would be great." His home was just a few streets away from our school. I told the other teacher and drove to his house. I parked in the driveway and walked very carefully on the snow. I went into their double carport to their side door. Christopher's mother opened the door, and there he stood, all bundled up head to toe and grinning. I took his mittened hand, and we began to go across the carport floor, which was icy. His little feet began slipping and sliding every which way. I was holding on tight so he couldn't fall. But his feet went backward then frontward. I said, "Christopher, I thought you wanted to go to school, or are you just going to skate all over your carport?" He was giggling the whole time his little feet were moving, every way.

Sometimes children really surprise you. Our art activity was a dot-to-dot banana. The children were to use a pencil to connect the dots and then color the banana yellow with a crayon. We had printed *banana* under the picture so the parents would know what it was. When you do dot-to-dot with four-year-olds, you have to erase their erratic lines and help them by placing your finger when they should draw to, step-by-step.

When we put the papers with their names printed at the top in front of them, one little blond-haired boy named Lance immediately said, "Oh, we're going to do a banana today."

I said, "How did you know?"

"Because," he answered, pointing to the word, "it says *banana* right here."

Carol and I looked at each other and said "*Wow!*" He could read many words at age four.

Some other unforgettable children were as follows:

Darren, Zarah, Kara, Ricky, PJ, Destiny, Dustin, Mary Elena, Caroline, Kendall, Blake, Mindy.

My heart hurt so much for a little boy named Austin. His mama had breast cancer and was fighting to live. She had prepared cupcakes and came to our classroom with all the party things. Mama's mother, Austin's grandmother, came to help her and see her precious little grandson enjoy his birthday celebration with his friends. He was so happy to see both of them. His birthday was of course physically tiring for his mama and her own mother. Austin's mama died just a few short weeks later. I think she knew it would be the last birthday celebration here. He finished the school year with us, and his daddy let him spend another year with us before he went on to kindergarten.

Many, many years before, Patrick and John had been in my class of four-year-olds. They were a year apart in age. Their mama died because of cancer. Their Aunt Susan (Mama's sister) and Uncle Rick took them in and adopted them. How blessed Patrick and John were and are!

Just a few years back, a little boy named Jedd spoke up one morning while we were having music. He said, "Ms. Hennis, can I sing a song we sing at my church?"

"Sure," I answered.

Jedd stood up and sang, "God's not dead. He's surely alive. He's living on the inside roaring like a lion. He's roaring, roaring like a lion."

His Mama would have been proud. And his pastor and the Newsboys.

Some other children were named Branson, Cambree, Mason, Audrey, Carleigh, Jaelind, Cal, Lane, Cameron.

I think of some children not only for their sweet ways but also for their deep voices, like Ashley (girl) and Morgan (boy). They both stole your heart right away.

There were two pictures I carried in my lesson plan notebook. The first one was Jesus, our loving, gentle Shepherd kneeling and reaching into the thicket of briars to take a little lamb who is so entangled that without escape, it would die there, without food and water. Didn't you know that briars tore Jesus's hands as He worked to free the helpless lamb? As the briars tore His hands to bleed, He did not stop until His little one was free and safe. He gently carried the lamb in His arms back where the flock was. Jesus would have applied healing oil to the lamb's wounds.

And then He put the lamb down, close to the rest of the flock, who were eating the tender grass and drinking from the cool water of the gently moving stream. You see, Jesus, the Good Shepherd, took the sheep where they needed to go. When the lamb was safe, then Jesus would have applied the healing oil to His own hands. I believe He thought of the time to come when His hands would be torn by the nails that would be hammered into them—*for you, for me*. Praise His wonderful name!

The second picture I carried in my nursery school lesson plan notebook showed a beautiful sunset over a mountain range. The caption across the bottom read, "God will move mountains. If you bring the shovel."

I have seen Him move mountains in the nursery school and in my own personal life. Thank you, Father!

"The joy of the Lord is my strength." Nehemiah wrote it. He lived it. So do I and every true follower of Jesus.

I pray this book will draw you closer to Jesus. And when it does, it will also draw you closer to all those you love. Filling you up with goodness and mercy that will follow you all the days of your life. The Good Shepherd promises this in His Holy Bible, the twenty-third psalm, "And He never fails to keep His promises." You are smiling as you read this, or you are yearning for it. If you are smiling, Jesus is your Savior, and you are safe as He leads you. If you are yearning to have that peace, just bow your head now and talk to Him. He is waiting with love unending and mercy to forgive all your sins. Trust Him. No one has ever loved you as much as He does.

Whatever briar thicket you are caught in, whether it be an addiction to alcohol, drugs, infidelity that destroys a marriage and family, gambling, pornography, homosexuality. You can die in that sin, or you can call out to Jesus. He's waiting. He loves you.

I've learned so much during my years at nursery school. I've been blessed with the love of the children. How I cherish that and the enduring friendships of their families, the parents, grandparents, aunts, uncles, and yes, the babysitters too. I hope every girl and every boy who went out our door was thinking, *Mrs. Hennis loves me.* I hope they all thought they were my favorite. Oh, they were! But more important, I hope they give Jesus their hearts and lives. I want to see them all in heaven.

On our family get-acquainted night meeting, I would say to the parents, "Look around this room. Your child's future in-laws could be sitting here. There are several young couples, happily married, living here in our area who first met the love of their life right here in this room." God has done amazing things here in all our lives, the little children, their families, and each of us teachers.

There were so many beautiful princesses and sweet little Mamas strolling their babies in carriages, so many little teachers holding books and reading to their class, and little chefs cooking and serving wonderful-tasting food. There were so many little Batman and Spiderman out to save the day, so many little farmers busy rounding up the cows that got out, so many little construction workers building skyscrapers and castles with four-year-old hands and blocks.

They will build tomorrow—the families, the homes, the cities, the countryside, the farms, the schools, the hospitals, the churches. Let us do our part to help them see that God has a wonderful plan for their future. He will help them find it and give them all they need to achieve it.

I want to give praise and honor to God, my Father, the giver of all things good and perfect. I want to give thanks that will never end to my precious Savior, Jesus Christ, for dying to save me. Thank you for my son, Chris, my daughter, Ann. I have loved them with every ounce of my being. Through the experiences of their lives, I've been drawn ever closer to God and Jesus. And then He gave the amazing gift of grandchildren, Michael, Andrew, Faith, and Kenzi. During the time Ann and Chris were young, I began working in the nursery school, and God has given me hundreds and hundreds more children to love and teach. How sweet is that!

About the Author

re you thinking about the legacy you are leaving behind? Be grateful for all that you've been given. Say it. Smile at others; they may need it. Help everyone you can.

Once, I was passing out cupcakes for a holiday party at First United Methodist Church Nursery School in Galax, Virginia. The boys and girls were seated at our three tables, all twenty-five of them. One little girl spoke up, saying, "You know what you are, Mrs. Hennis? You are a servant."

I answered, "You are right, sweetie. I am. I am serving you and all of your friends because I love you. That's what a servant does."

The parts of my life that I treasure most have been with children. Oh, I have many adult friends of all ages and races and both sexes who mean so much to me. But no one fills my heart to over-flowing like the children do. God gave me the sweetest work to do.

Like the song says, "Love in your heart wasn't put there to stay. Love isn't love till you give it away."

CPSIA information can be obtained
at www.ICGtesting.com
Printed in the USA
BVHW022114300620
582434BV00002B/5